WEREWOLF M

Pack Law 4

Becca Van

MENAGE EVERLASTING

Siren Publishing, Inc.
www.SirenPublishing.com

A SIREN PUBLISHING BOOK
IMPRINT: Ménage Everlasting

WEREWOLF MATES
Copyright © 2012 by Becca Van

ISBN: 978-1-62241-665-3

First Printing: October 2012

Cover design by Les Byerley
All art and logo copyright © 2012 by Siren Publishing, Inc.

Printed in the U.S.A.

PUBLISHER
Siren Publishing, Inc.
www.SirenPublishing.com

DEDICATION

To anyone who needs to escape reality for a while. Enjoy!

WEREWOLF MATES

Pack Law 4

BECCA VAN
Copyright © 2012

Chapter One

Samantha Winters felt eyes on her, and the hair on her nape stood on end. *Where is that coming from?* She didn't dare glance around the small-town diner, afraid that she would turn on her stool and come face-to-face with Gerard.

He can't have followed me. The last place she thought she'd seen him was at the New Mexico border. Filling her rusted-out bomb with gas that she could barely afford, she'd thought she saw the shifty bastard on the other side of the pumps. Even as she told herself she was just being paranoid, she'd ripped out of that station so fast she was surprised she hadn't melted the asphalt behind her. Not until arriving at the outskirts of Aztec did she let her foot up off the gas.

Now she wasn't so sure she'd just been succumbing to paranoia. The sensation at the back of her neck wasn't going away.

She finished her coffee and left money on the counter for the bill. She hesitated for a moment as she sifted through her last remaining dollars, but in the end she left the tip the waitress deserved. Having waited tables herself, she knew how much tips mattered, and at this point it didn't matter how much Samantha tried to hoard her pennies. She was going to be out of cash soon.

As she left the diner, her eyes took note of the shops lining the main street of Aztec, but she was also aware of the people around her as they went about their business. She still couldn't shake the feeling of being watched. She had thought she was safe here, so far away from her hometown of Sebring, Florida.

She decided to step into a store. If anyone was following her, maybe she could give them the slip. Glancing up, she saw a doorway and, beyond it, racks of clothes. She darted inside without a second thought.

The sales clerk gave her a slightly cool welcome accompanied by a dubious once-over. Samantha wasn't wearing anything half as fancy as these clothes, but she gave the clerk a smile and went to the rack near the front windows. While her hands sifted through the clothes on the rack, her eyes watched the pavement through the window. Beyond the well-dressed mannequin, pedestrians passed in both directions, but she saw no one suspicious.

Being on the road for so long was getting to her. Between her weariness and the financial strain of being on the run, she wondered if maybe she ought to hang out in Aztec for a little while. All she really needed was to find a job.

Samantha warmed to the idea. Maybe she could even work here. Her gaze went to the jacket she'd been pretending to examine. *I can see myself wearing something like this.*

Then she flipped over the price tag. She let go of the jacket like it had burned her.

Hazarding a glance over her shoulder, she found the sales clerk watching her through narrowed eyes. Samantha felt her cheeks burn. Squeaking a thank-you to the clerk, she went back outside.

The prickling on her neck had relented inside the store, but now it was back. Feeling more unnerved than ever, she stood on the sidewalk and tried to figure out who was giving her that feeling. *Kids walking home from school? No. Mailman? Nope.*

Samantha looked directly to her right and froze.

Gorgeous guy standing by a tree?

About twenty feet down the sidewalk, a very tall man wearing a black T-shirt was fiddling with his cell. At least, he was now. Samantha was almost certain that a moment before she'd set her eyes on him, he'd been watching her.

She put her back to him and made for her motel. Hurrying down the street to the room she had booked a couple of hours ago, she knew she wouldn't feel safe again until she was behind a closed, locked door. But the feeling she was getting now wasn't exactly fear. She wanted to look over her shoulder and see the tall guy again. The idea that he might be following her should have been scary, but she found it strangely comforting.

Girl, you're losing your mind. The last thing she needed right now was anyone following her, tall and good looking or not.

Back in her room, she crept to the curtain-covered window and peered out into the parking lot of the motel but couldn't see anything.

Sighing, she moved over to the bed and sat down. That moment of feeling watched and protected had fled. Now she just felt watched and scared again.

God, what am I going to do now? I have only a few dollars left and am down to the last quarter tank of gas.

Sam spied the local paper on the coffee table in the room and picked it up. She flicked the pages open until she found the employment section and started to peruse the classifieds. There wasn't much in the paper she was capable of doing, since she only had supermarket, waitressing, and bartending experience, but she was determined to find something before the day was out. She had to, otherwise she would have to take to living in her car and going hungry. A giggle of hysteria rose in her chest and burst out from between her lips. Sliding sideways on the small sofa she was seated on, she curled into a ball and clutched her knees to her chest until the laughter gave way to great wracking sobs. Her life was a mess, she was a mess, and she had no one to turn to for help.

* * * *

His wolf howled and then shivered beneath his skin then butted against him, trying to get out. The beast wanted total reign over him as he scented the woman he had been waiting for since he knew what a mate was. He inhaled deeply as a tantalizing scent assailed his nostrils when he stepped outside of the Aztec Club after finishing his shift behind the bar. Never had Roan smelled such an intoxicating aroma, and he grinned as the image of a cartoon character floating in the air as he followed a scent trail flashed through his mind. He wanted to wrap himself in that perfume, roll around and drench his wolf-body in it until his wolf was satisfied, but of course he couldn't. For one, he didn't want anyone beside his pack members knowing he was a werewolf, and two, he would definitely cause a stir amongst the human citizens of Aztec, New Mexico, if he stripped down to his bare skin and ended up arrested for indecent exposure in the middle of town.

Drawing the aroma into his nose and filling his lungs with the essence, he turned to follow that amazing fragrance. He couldn't even begin to describe how that scent made him feel. It was fresh and sweet, making his cock stand at attention. His heartbeat picked up and his breathing escalated. Goose bumps rose up on his skin, the hair on his body standing up alertly, but not because of any danger. It was like his whole body was being drawn toward the perfume like a magnet, and he had no desire to resist that call.

The sweet bouquet led Roan to the small diner, and he entered with heartfelt purpose. He scanned the interior, calling on his inner beast to find his quarry but being careful not to reveal his animal. The last thing he wanted was for someone to notice his eyes changing from their usual brown color to a glowing gold. He found her sitting at the long counter drinking coffee and was blown away at first sight.

She was absolutely gorgeous. With long brown hair and smooth, white, creamy skin, she was petite and small in stature, but she had curves in all the right places. He could only see a partial profile, but from what he could see of her lips, oh man, he had to stop himself from going up to her and tasting those full, lush, and naturally red cupid bows.

Stalking toward the empty stool beside her, he took a seat, and even though he wanted to turn and stare at her, to take in her features until he had every minute detail burned into his brain, he restrained himself. Not wanting to scare her off with his intensity, Roan ordered a coffee and was only vaguely aware of the elderly waitress leaving to get his drink. Keeping his head facing straight ahead, he surreptitiously watched her out of the corner of his eye from beneath slightly lowered lashes.

He wanted to know everything about her. Where she came from, what her name was, what her favorite color was, if she was staying in Aztec, and if so for how long. He wanted to breathe her in and keep her by his side until he was permanently etched into her heart, body, and soul. He wanted to pick her up and take her back to the den and then bury himself in that small, lush body until neither of them could walk.

But he knew if he told her what he was feeling she would likely run screaming from him with horror or look at him like he was delusional. Humans sometimes had a hard time with the idea of being mated to three men, let alone werewolves. He followed after a few minutes and kept her in his sights. Hiding behind a thick tree trunk, he studied her intently.

She ducked into a store then reappeared moments later. She hesitated on the sidewalk. His mate looked so upset. Had that sales clerk given her shit? If so, Roan would give her a piece of his mind. His mate turned toward him, and his enhanced sight caught the shimmer of tears in her eyes. He wanted to rush over to her and enfold her in his arms, wanted to offer her comfort. He wanted to know what made her so sad and what had caused the pain in her eyes.

Roan followed her until she entered a room in the new Aztec Motel. Sighing with resignation, he turned on his heel and hurried back toward his car, which he had left outside of the Aztec Club. He needed to see his brothers and let them know he had found their mate.

Roan got into his car and, instead of driving toward the pack house, eased out of the parking lot and headed toward the Aztec Motel. The thought of leaving his mate when she might disappear was too much to bear. He parked his car and sat watching her door.

Heaving another sigh, he knew he couldn't delay any longer. He was going to need his brothers' help if they were going to have a chance with their mate. *"Chet, Justin, I have found our mate,"* Roan said through their personal mind link. *"She's holed up in the Aztec Motel, where I'm currently sitting in my car."*

"How do you know for sure she's our mate?" asked Chet.

"You wouldn't ask me that if you'd smelled her scent or had to control your beast from trying to claim her."

"What does she look like?" Justin inquired.

"Oh man, she's beautiful. She has long brown hair, the sweetest brown eyes, and mmm-hmm, curves just begging to be caressed. From what I could tell, her ass is a ripe peach just begging to have a bite taken out of it, and even though she's not very tall, boy does she had a set of legs on her."

"Do you know where she's from?" Chet asked.

"No. I didn't get a chance to talk to her. I found her in the diner, and she left a minute after I arrived. I followed her to the motel."

"Shit, Roan, what if she's only stopped for the night? How the hell are we going to get her to stay?" Justin queried.

"I don't know. I haven't worked that out yet."

"It's a pity she didn't take a room at the club. We could have watched her from there. You can't stay in the motel parking lot all night. You'll cause suspicion," Chet speculated.

"What the hell do you want me to do? I'm not leaving. She could check out at any time."

"We'll figure that out if it happens," Justin replied. *"Once we get there, we can form a plan."*

"Good. So, how long before you get here?"

"We're already on our way. We should be there in twenty minutes."

"Did you inform the Alphas? And don't forget to bring me some clothes."

"Already taken care of."

Roan figured his brothers must have begun preparations as soon as he told them about their mate. The three of them had all been restless since the Alphas of Friess Pack had found their mate. And then one after the other, the Betas, the second layer of pack hierarchy, had found their mates as well. As he watched their cousins the Domain brothers and both sets of Friess brothers find their mates, Roan had felt divided between happiness and envy. It was so hard watching his family claim the one true female meant for them, since he and his brothers were still waiting for their own mate. The yearning to have the love of his life in his arms had been there for a long time, but as each of his family members found their own woman, it had made him realize how lonely he truly was.

One night he had heard his pack leaders and Beta cousins talking about the way their werewolf powers had been enhanced once they had claimed their mates. It seemed their already-augmented hearing, sight, strength, and speed increased even further, but he couldn't fathom such a thing. Being werewolves, he and the members of the pack already had phenomenal strength compared to the average human male. Roan and his brothers would experience the same increase in strength if they persuaded their woman to mate with them. But there was a long way to go before he could imagine that happening.

The powers were a bonus, but they weren't the real reason Roan longed to go into her room and pull her into his arms. To wrap her in his love and protection. He and his brothers wanted to have a woman in their lives to love and nurture. To fill the empty places in their hearts only a mate ever could.

Roan sat up straight in his seat when the door to his woman's room opened. There she was. God, she was beautiful. The setting sun shone down on her head as she walked toward the reception office of the motel, and he could see red and blonde strands of hair highlighted throughout her tresses as the ends caressed the top of her ass. What he wouldn't give to be able to run his fingers through that mane and see if it was as soft as it looked. Groaning with arousal, imagining that hair sweeping across his thighs and cock, he adjusted his hard dick. He wanted to wrap those strands around his wrist and hold her steady as he fucked her mouth. Taking a deep breath to control his raging libido and his persistent wolf, who was once again pushing at him to make a claim, he shifted in his seat and got out of his truck.

As soon as he stepped into the office, her scent wrapped around him once more, taking his breath away. He sidled up to her and listened as she conversed with the elderly woman behind the counter. She was asking about employment. Joy filled his heart, because if she found work, that meant she was going to be staying in Aztec, at least for a while.

"No, I'm sorry. I don't have any positions available right now," the elderly woman replied.

"Well, thanks anyway," his mate said.

Roan couldn't let such an opportunity pass him by, so when she began to turn to head out, he quickly sidestepped, and she bumped right into him.

"Oh, sorry, I didn't see you standing there," she apologized.

Fuck. Her voice had a low, husky cadence which immediately put his mind in the gutter. He wondered if it would go lower when she was aroused or on the verge of climax. And her eyes were what he thought would be called bedroom eyes. Her lids looked like they were half-closed, the dark, sooty lashes giving her a sensual appeal, and her irises were a deep, soulful brown.

"No problem," he rasped. "I couldn't help overhearing that you're looking for work. I have a job you may be interested in."

"Oh?"

"My name is Roan Domain, and I work at the Aztec Club down the street. We have need for a waitperson if you're interested. Room and board are provided in the package," he stated, extending his hand to her.

She took his proffered hand, and he saw those sexy eyelids flicker up. Her eyes seemed to light from within, and her pupils dilated slightly. Tugging her hand away from him as if he'd burned her, she licked her lips nervously, drawing his gaze to her mouth, and took a quick step back.

Oh yeah. She'd felt it, too. That little zing of electricity which had passed between them. His nostrils flared as his wolf picked up her scent of arousal and began butting at him from inside.

"Samantha Winters, but call me Sam," she stated in a deep, husky voice, which grabbed hold of his cock, making it pulse against his zipper.

"Why don't we go on over to the club and get some dinner? We can talk about the particulars, and you can ask what you want to know," Roan suggested.

"Um, uh…sure."

"Change of plans, guys. I've just made contact and offered her a job at the club. She's coming to have dinner there with me to talk over the particulars," Roan explained.

"We're nearly there. We were just about to pass by," Chet replied. *"We'll grab our usual table."*

"She's nervous, so take it easy on her, Justin," Roan commanded.

"I'm not stupid, Roan. I'm not going to boss her around."

"Yeah well, that might be easier said than done, bro. Once she's near, your wolf is gonna want to take over. And since you're the eldest and the most dominant, I just want you to be prepared."

"Just shut up and get over here," Jason demanded with a growl.

"See, that's what I'm talking about. You need to back off tonight."

"Yeah, yeah."

Roan stepped up closer to Sam and took her elbow in his hand. She had to tilt her head back to look up at him, and he could see the apprehension in her gaze when her eyes connected with his.

"Come on, Samantha. Let's go get some food," Roan said and guided her out to his truck. Opening the passenger door, he noticed her eyeing the high step. Not giving her a chance to protest, he clasped her waist and lifted her onto the seat.

"Thanks," she said in a higher-pitched voice.

"You're welcome." Roan closed the door and walked around to the truck, inhaling as much fresh air as he could so he could try and suppress his raging arousal. It was going to be pure torture in the confined space of his vehicle. The last thing he wanted was for his eyes to begin glowing in her vicinity.

Chapter Two

Sam wondered how she had ended up sitting between two tall, muscular, hunky men with another sitting across from her.

Roan had led her to a booth in the back of the club and introduced her to his brothers, Justin and Chet. Even though she was wary of them, she felt drawn to these men as well. When she had shaken both their hands, the zap of electricity she had felt with their brother had coursed through her body again. First Justin and then Chet had perused her body from head to toe, causing cream to leak from her pussy and her clit to throb. She had tried to withdraw from them and kept her voice cool, hoping they didn't realize how they all affected her. But she was having a hard time hiding her arousal, and the sexual tension was so thick she could have cut it with a knife.

No matter how sexy the three of them were, though, she doubted she would even have given Roan the time of day if she hadn't been so desperate for a job. She was over men and the way they treated women, and she'd had enough of the opposite sex to last her a lifetime. But these three men kept drawing her eyes back to them again and again.

Shit, Roan was so damn hot, with his shoulder-length black hair and brown eyes. As she was short, his height of six two made her feel small and petite. She had never thought about how she felt next to tall men until now, when she was surrounded by them. Roan had wide shoulders which tapered down to a slim, taut abdomen and hips with long, lithe legs and looked strong and muscular in a rangy, athletic type of way.

His brother, Chet, looked to be the youngest of the three but also the tallest at about six foot six. He moved to the end of his seat and stood, staring at her. She slid her gaze away, in case he thought she was ogling him, to where she wrung her fingers and glanced upward at him through her lashes. His tight T-shirt accentuated the rippling muscles beneath the cotton as he shifted, and he looked at her expectantly. His hair was a dark brown, almost the color of chocolate, and his eyes were hazel, a mix of green with brown and gold flecks.

"What would you like to drink, darlin'?" Chet asked.

Goose bumps rose on her skin as the deep cadence of his voice washed over her, and she squirmed in her seat when her pussy clenched and leaked juices onto her panties. *God, Sam, what the hell? You've only just met these men and your body's ripening from the sound of their voices. Get a grip, girl!*

"W–Water, please," she answered, hearing the breathless quality of her voice, and lowered her eyes again quickly.

Shifting her eyes to Justin, her breath caught in her throat. His irises were a deep, stormy gray, and he was looking at her as if he wanted to devour her whole. His hair was dark enough to be almost black, but she could see traces of brown throughout. His shoulders were very wide, his biceps looked to be larger than she would be able to encompass with two hands, and he was packed full of rippling muscles. She didn't think he was as tall as Chet or shorter than Roan in height, but until she saw him standing she wouldn't be sure.

Quickly diverting her eyes to her lap again, she tried to get her wayward mind and body to return from what she considered freakish reactions to three strangers.

The three Domain brothers seemed to be a fair bit older than her twenty-three years, and she felt as if she was out of her element considering they appeared to be in their early to mid thirties.

"What do you want to eat, sweetness?" Roan whispered in her ear, and she sucked in a gasp when his hot, moist breath caressed her flesh.

"Uh…pardon?" she asked. Even though she had heard and understood the question, she wanted a little more time to get her body back under control, and she hadn't even looked at the menu, which sat in the middle of the table. *And what's with all the endearments? I don't even know these men.*

"Food, Sam. What do you want?"

"A burger," she blurted and felt heat rise in her cheeks. *God, Sam, could you be any gawkier?*

"A girl after my own heart," Justin stated from her other side. He must have shifted closer to her, because she could feel the heat emanating from his body, and his masculine scent assailed her nostrils. The smell of his sweat was so nice mixed in with spicy soap and clean male. It was so enticing she couldn't help taking a deep breath for another whiff.

"How do you want your burger, sweetness?"

"Pardon?" Sam asked, looking up at Roan.

"Do you want a cheeseburger or one with the works, Sam?"

"With the works, please," she replied just as Chet returned to their table.

Gratefully reaching for the glass of water, she downed half the contents in one go and only looked up when she realized silence reigned around her immediate vicinity.

"Do you want another of those, darlin'?" Chet asked.

"No, thank you. I'm fine."

Roan touched her arm to draw her attention but held a finger up when the waitress came to take their order. Once the waitress was gone again, he turned back to her.

"We could use another waitress here, sweetness. Do you think you'd be interested?"

"Yes. I've worked as a check-out chick, bartender, and waitress."

"Well, you sound like you're exactly what we need," Justin said. "You realize that room and meals are included in the package."

"That seems to be very generous," Sam said hesitantly.

"We like to take care of our employees, honey. Our cousins own this establishment and like to know that the people they employ are going to hang around for a while," Justin stated firmly.

Sam could tell he wanted an affirmation that she would hang around, too, but she couldn't make a promise she might break. So she lowered her eyes and didn't confirm or deny his unspoken question.

"Where are you from, Sam?" Chet asked, breaking into the uncomfortable silence.

"Florida."

"What brings you to this neck of the woods?" Justin asked.

"Um, I–I just felt like a change," she answered, shifting uncomfortably.

"Are you married, sweetness?" Roan asked, and when she looked up she saw he was looking at her bare left ring finger.

"Divorced," she replied abruptly, not wanting to get into the particulars of her farcical marriage. If she opened her mouth to explain, she was scared the whole sordid story would come spilling out, and the last thing she needed was to see their pity at her predicament.

"So, when can you start, honey?" Justin asked.

"What?"

"When can you start working at the club?" he asked again.

"Oh, tomorrow, if that's what you want. Are you sure you don't have to check with the owners before you hire me?"

"No, darlin', we are running the club right now. Our cousins have more important things to oversee at the moment. If they didn't trust us, we wouldn't have complete control," Chet explained. "And yes, you can start tomorrow. Does three o'clock suit you?"

"Yes, that's fine. What do you all want me to do?"

"You can help out wherever you're needed," Roan answered. "Do you have any experience cooking, sweetheart?"

"Um, yes, I often helped cook in the last hotel I worked for. I love to cook. I had planned on being a chef, but things didn't work out,"

Sam explained and then cursed at her runaway mouth. She hadn't meant to reveal anything about herself, but there was nothing she could do since the horse had already bolted.

"Why didn't you, honey?" asked Justin.

"Um." Sam began scrabbling in her mind for something to say without going into too much detail, and then she sighed with relief when the waitress brought their order.

"Shelley, this here is Samantha Winters." Chet introduced her to the waitress. "She'll be starting work here tomorrow."

"Hi, Samantha, welcome aboard," Shelley said and gave her a wink.

"Nice to meet you." She then looked at the massive burger on the plate in front of her. Her stomach was all tied up in knots she was so nervous, and she didn't know if she could stomach any food right now, but she didn't want to appear rude after the trouble the three Domain brothers had gone to by hiring her and ordering her dinner.

She cut the hamburger in four and picked up a quarter. Taking a bite, she looked up as she chewed. They were all staring at her again. Chet caught her eye, and the corner of his mouth tilted up in a sexy half grin, but she hastily looked away again.

By the time the three men had finished eating Sam had only done justice to quarter of the burger but couldn't have taken another bite.

"Are you all right, Sam?" Roan asked.

"Yes," she answered and looked up at him. He had a frown on his face, and he was looking at her as if he were worried about her. *Don't be stupid, Samantha. The man doesn't even know you, so why would he worry for you? He's just being polite because you didn't eat much.*

"If you're finished, why don't we help you pack up your stuff and move you in upstairs?" Chet inquired.

"Oh, I had thought I could move in tomorrow morning sometime. I've already paid for tonight's accommodation at the motel."

"Okay. What time do you want to move tomorrow, honey?" Justin queried. "We'll be there to give you a hand."

"You don't need to do that. I only have a couple of bags." She turned to look at him.

Staring into his eyes she thought she saw his irises flash from gray to gold and back again. The hair on her nape stood on end, but when she blinked, his eyes looked normal and all expression was wiped from his face. Turning back to Chet when he spoke, she caught him glaring at Justin just before he pinned her with his gaze.

"Would you like another drink, darlin'?"

"Yes, please. How long have you lived in Aztec?" she asked, directing her question to Roan.

"We were born here, sweetness. Our family has been in this town for generations."

"Wow, it must be nice to have such sturdy roots."

"What about you, honey? Where in Florida did you grow up?" Justin asked, taking the bottle of beer Chet handed him when he returned to the table.

"I spent my childhood in Sebring."

"Do you have any brothers or sisters, darlin'?" Chet inquired.

"No."

"And your parents, do they still live in Sebring?" asked Justin.

"No, my parents are no longer living. They died six months before I finished high school," she replied emotionlessly.

"Shit, that must have been hard on you, Sam," Roan said gently.

"I survived. I finished school and was able to continue paying the mortgage with the small life insurance policy my dad had. Then I sold up, intending to use the remaining proceeds from the sale to go to culinary school."

"But you didn't go, did you, honey." Justin took hold of her hand. "What happened?"

Sam opened her mouth to answer automatically and then quickly closed it again. She didn't want them to know how gullible she had been, but the urge to blurt out what a mess her life was in was nearly tangible. How long had it been since she had someone to lean on?

Chapter Three

Justin knew she was leaving out a huge amount of information. He wanted to ask her so many questions, to find out why she looked so sad, lonely, and scared, but he didn't want to frighten her off. She hadn't stopped fidgeting and squirming since she sat down, and she'd hardly touched her food. In his opinion she could definitely do with another few pounds on her slim frame, but he didn't have the right to make sure she was eating properly, at least not yet.

Roan had been right. Samantha Winters was their mate, and he intended to do anything he could to keep her in Aztec and woo her into their beds. She was such a timid little thing, but man was she a looker. He had already figured out she had a submissive nature and couldn't wait to test her mettle. Everyone had a limit, and he wondered how far he could push before she reached hers. Nearly every time she met his gaze, her eyes skittered away and looked down. She had avoided looking at his brothers too much, too. But underlying all that nervous energy he could smell her arousal. He'd caught her giving them all the once-over and hoped she liked what she saw, because he definitely did. If the scent emanating from her pussy was any indication, she was definitely attracted to them.

"Could you let me out, please?" she asked Roan.

"You haven't finished your drink yet, sweetness." He indicated her untouched soda.

"I need the ladies' room," she replied haughtily.

And just like that, some of her true nature shone through. Justin smiled over her head at Roan and then Chet. He could see their eyes twinkling with amusement, too, and knew that they liked that she had some backbone at least. When she was on her way to the bathroom, Roan slid back into the booth.

"Well, what did I tell you? She's our mate, isn't she?"

"Yes, she's ours," Justin growled possessively.

"Fuck, Justin. You're going to have to watch it. Your eyes began to change, and Sam noticed," Chet said.

"Yeah, I know. Sorry, but fuck, she's such a submissive little thing, she brings the beast out in me."

"I don't think she's as passive as she makes out. She told you just a minute ago," Chet said, pointing at Roan.

"Yeah." He sighed wistfully. "Who would have thought such a husky voice could sound so cool?"

"So what do you think her story is?"

"I don't know, but she's scared of something."

"Do you think she's running from her ex?" Chet queried.

"Could be, but we won't know for sure until she opens up with us."

"She's not going to do that yet. She's so fucking skittish she can't sit still," Chet explained.

"Yeah and every time she moves my wolf gets a whiff of that sweet pussy cream," Roan groaned.

"I can't wait to get between those slender thighs. I could feast on that sweet little cunt for hours," Chet rasped.

"She's taking too long," Justin interrupted. "She should have been back by now."

"Fuck! You don't think she's made a run for it, do you?" Chet rose to his feet.

"No." Justin sniffed the air. "She's in the back corridor and she's scared. Move!"

Justin, Roan, and Chet hurried through the tables and people until they were at the entrance to the dimly lit corridor which led to the restrooms. A rumbling growl started low in Justin's chest, and the hair on his nape stood on end. Their mate was currently trying to push through two human males as they caged her against the wall.

Justin didn't even realize that he'd moved until his hand wrapped around the nape of one man as he heard Samantha asking to be released.

"The lady asked you to let her go. Didn't your momma teach you any manners?"

"Hey! Who the fuck do you think you are? Back off, man."

Justin turned his back toward Sam so she wouldn't see his face and let the bastard see the full force of his angry wolf. He bared his teeth and let his eyes change from their normal gray to golden fury.

"What the fuck! Uh, hey, sorry, man, I didn't know she was with you," the idiot whined.

"It doesn't matter whether she is or not. You shouldn't be treating her that way. Women are to be looked after, not accosted or abused," Justin spat out. "Leave and don't come back. If I catch you, or your friend, anywhere near this town again, there'll be trouble."

"Sure, whatever you say. We were just leaving."

Justin watched the two men until he saw them leave the club and then turned back to face Samantha. She was currently sandwiched between Roan and Chet, her head hiding against Chet's chest.

"Are you okay, honey? Did they hurt you?" Justin asked.

"No," came her muffled reply, and then she lifted her head. Her cheeks were pale, her pupils were dilated, and he could see the slight tremors wracking her small frame. "They didn't hurt me. They were just out to start trouble. Thanks for coming to my rescue."

Justin was about to pull her out of his brothers' arms and into his own, but she buried her face again and he heard her sniffle. *Shit.* She was crying. Those two fuckers had really scared her. He frowned over her reaction. He could understand her being nervous and angry, but Samantha was terrified. *"What the hell is going on?"*

"I don't know, bro, but she's shaking like a leaf," Chet replied.

"Shh, it's okay, sweetness. They're gone now. We won't let anyone hurt you," Roan said as he caressed her back.

"Do you think her husband abused her?" Chet asked.

"I don't know, but I intend to find out," Justin answered firmly. "Sam, come here, honey."

She peeked up at him, and when he saw tears sparkling on her lashes and the wet trail down her cheeks, he wanted to track those two pricks and rip out their throats. Taking a deep breath to control his anger, which he knew was an overreaction to her fear, he pushed those thoughts aside.

Moving slowly, so as not to startle her, he took hold of her hand and pulled her into his side. Wrapping an arm around her shoulders, he led her to the doorway halfway down the hall, opened the door, and stepped into the office. Roan and Chet followed and closed the door behind them.

He walked her over to the couch, sat down, and pulled her onto his thighs. Expecting her to make a fuss and push away from him, he was surprised when she turned her head and hid her face between his pecs. God, she felt so right, on his lap and in his arms.

"I can understand you being afraid of strange men coming on to you, honey, but why were you so scared? What's going on, Sam?"

"I don't want to talk about it," she replied, her forehead still nestled into his chest.

"Sweetness, we only want to help you. Are you in trouble, Sam?" Roan asked as he sat down beside them.

"I don't know."

"What do you mean by that, darlin'?" Chet inquired from his position, leaning against the desk across the room.

She didn't answer this time, just gave a shrug of her shoulders. Justin had had enough of her trying to hide from them, so he placed an arm beneath her knees and a hand between her shoulder blades to keep her steady and shifted her around on his lap. When he had her back cradled in the crook of his arm, he took her chin between his index finger and thumb, turning her head so her eyes met his.

"Answer the questions, Sam. Are you or are you not in trouble?" he demanded to know.

"I was, but I ran." She tried to pull her chin from his hand. Letting her go, he placed his hand around her throat, holding her lightly, caressing her soft, silky skin with his thumb. Hearing her breath hitch in her chest, he let go immediately. The last thing he wanted was to have her scared of him.

"Tell me," Justin commanded.

"I don't want to talk about it right now," Sam stated with a haughty tilt to her chin.

Justin's wolf pushed against him, wanting to make her submit to him because of her little action of aggression and defiance. He inhaled through his nose and knew instantly that was a mistake. Her sweet scent wrapped around him, making his wolf howl inside, begging him to claim her. She smelled of oranges, peaches, and feminine arousal. He closed his eyes both to regain dominance over his inner beast and to hide his irises in case they began to glow gold. He pushed back hard against his wolf. When he felt it was once again safe, he opened his eyes to look down at her.

"All right, I'll leave it be for now, but don't think you can hide from us too long, honey. I will get the answers I want."

Samantha pushed off his lap, and he reluctantly let her go. Standing before them, her head lowered, she wrung her hands together, but when she lifted her head there was fire buried in the depths of her eyes.

"I really should be going now. Thank you for the job and dinner," she said, edging toward the door.

"I'll drive you back, sweetheart." Roan stood and moved toward her.

"Oh, you don't have to do that. It's not too far to walk, and I don't want to be a bother."

"Do you honestly think we are going to let you walk back to the motel, alone, in the dark, after what just happened? You aren't a bother, honey. Let Roan drive you back," Justin stated firmly.

Expressions flittered across her face. First there was nervousness, anger, then fear, and finally relieved resignation.

"Okay, thank you again. It was nice meeting you all," she said quietly and opened the door. She left without a backward glance, Roan following behind her.

"Do you want me to get Chris, Blayk, and James to run a check on her?" Chet asked.

Justin pondered whether his aforementioned cousins, who happened to be the heads of security of the Friess Pack, should look into Samantha's background. Even though the thought was tempting, he really wanted to give her the chance to open up to them on her own.

"No, not yet. Let's give her some time to get used to us first. Yes, she's submissive to a point and running scared from something, but she also trusts us. Give her a little more time and I think she'll trust us even more."

"Why do you think she trusts us?"

"Because she didn't try to leave even though she was nervous, and she didn't try to push us away when we protected her. She snuggled into Roan as if she had known him for years, even when she was scared of those two idiots. And she didn't protest when I pulled her onto my lap."

"Hmm, you may be right. We'll ease her into wanting to be around us, and then, God willing, she'll want to mate with us when the time is right. Fuck! How do you think she's going to react when she finds out we're werewolves?"

"That's the million dollar question, isn't it?" Justin smiled wryly as he stared at the door she'd left through only minutes earlier.

* * * *

He watched from behind the dark windows of his car and felt anger building up inside him. He snarled aloud. The man leading her to the motel room was holding her elbow as if he had the right to be possessive.

He recalled everything her weasel of a husband had told him about her. How she loved to be tied down and helpless during sex. The way she loved to be smacked around and got off when beaten during copulation turned him on more than anyone else ever had.

Just the thought of having her was enough to arouse him. He was about to pull his dick out from the material confines of his jeans when he saw the brute with her look toward him.

He didn't think he could be seen, but he felt uneasy when those eyes didn't waver away from his. Deciding caution was the better part of valor, he started his car and pulled out of the parking lot. Looking back in the rearview mirror just before he was out of view, his gaze connected with the man's once more. He was going to have to be very careful to avoid that man. He didn't like the feeling of being prey one little bit.

Chapter Four

Roan felt his hackles rise and heard a growl of anger coming from a car hidden in the shadows of the parking lot. He turned toward the sound and, using his wolf vision, pinned the man in the vehicle with his gaze. The bastard looked to be watching Samantha, and Roan could feel the fury rolling off him in waves.

When the car started and peeled out of the parking lot, Roan knew his assumption had been correct. Whoever that man was, he had been watching his mate and had thought he was safe until Roan heard and spotted him.

His mate had someone trailing her. The desire to know she was safe and protected clawed at his insides with possessiveness. There was no way he was leaving her alone when she could be in danger.

"You need to pack a bag, sweetness. It's not safe for you here. I want you to come back to our family home where we can protect you," Roan stated firmly.

"What? What are you talking about?"

"The car that just left was occupied by a man, and he was watching you. I think it would be better for you to stay with us."

"I don't think that's such a good idea. Besides, how the hell could you see who was in the car? The windows were tinted, and it's as black as sin out tonight."

"I have excellent vision, Sam. Be a good girl and pack your bags. Whoever you're running from has found you."

Roan saw her shiver and knew he had finally succeeded in making her think about her own safety.

"I could just move to the club?" she asked more than stated. But he could hear the fear in her voice and wanted to protect her more than anything else right now.

"Well, you could, but there is no one else currently renting the rooms upstairs. I wouldn't feel right leaving you there by yourself. Anyone could break in and hurt you if that was their intention. We have our own suite of rooms in the house we share with our family, and you could bunk down in the spare room as long as you like."

"I'm really not sure I should…"

"Sweetheart, I'm not sure you understand the situation. Whoever that was watching you wasn't just out to enjoy the night air. Now, you have three choices. One, you can pack your things and come back home with us. Two, I can stay here with you, or three, I can summon Justin, and believe me, he won't give you a choice. So, what's it to be, Sam?"

She was nibbling on her lip and looking anywhere but at him. He could see the uncertainty in her face and the frown between her eyes. A need to reach out, to pull her into his arms and soothe that lip with his tongue before he plundered her mouth, grabbed him by the balls. Clenching his teeth and fisting his hands didn't help one little bit.

"Are you sure you have a spare room? And who do you all live with? What if they don't want me in your house?"

"First off, you will be welcomed by everyone. We have a large family, Sam, lots of cousins and such. Since we have all worked together to combine an entrepreneurial empire, we decided that living in the same house was the best option. Some of my cousins are into the security business. Others look after properties we've acquired, and others, such as ourselves, work wherever we're needed. You'll be able to meet all of my relatives but also the CEOs of our operation, Jonah, Mikhail, and Brock Friess, along with their wife, Michelle."

"Their wife! What do you mean by that?" Sam asked as she finally unlocked and pushed open the door to her room.

"Just what I said, sweetheart. Their wife. Our family is a little unconventional," Roan explained and the phrase "understatement of the century" drifted through his thoughts. "The men in our family tend to fall in love with the same woman, and if she is agreeable, she ends up in a relationship with them."

"What?" she asked incredulously.

"Shit. Sorry, Sam I don't mean that *all* the men in the family share the same woman. What I meant was that brothers seem to love the same woman. So far, my Al—ah, cousins Jonah, Mikhail, and Brock Friess are mate—married to Michelle. Greg, Jake, and Devon Domain are married to Keira, and Chris, Blayk, and James Friess are married to Talia."

"But how is that even possible? Last I heard, polygamy was against the law!" Sam exclaimed.

"It is, sweetheart. The woman marries the eldest male but is committed to the other men in her heart," Roan explained.

"Oh boy, when you said your family was a little unconventional, I had no idea how much."

You still don't, sweetheart. God, I wish I could tell you everything right now and then take you to bed and claim you. I want to see those sweet eyes glazed over with passion and to taste those sinful lips of yours. You have no idea how much I want to bury my cock into that sweet pussy and bite you so you will be by my side for the rest of your life.

Roan cleared his throat and pushed his thoughts aside. Thinking like that only seemed to rile his wolf, and that was the last thing he needed right now.

"You still haven't told me what you've decided, Sam. What's it going to be, sweetheart? Do I stay here with you or at the club, or are you going to come home with us?"

Once again Sam nibbled on her lip. Expressions flittered across her face as she tried to decide. Her face was very expressive, and he watched as first nervous apprehension skated over her features, then outright fear, and finally acquiescence. He held his breath, hardly daring to hope her decision was going to be what he wanted, but no matter what she said, he wasn't about to leave her side.

"I'll take you up on the offer of your spare room, but if we get there and I find you've lied to me, I will make you bring me back here straight away," she declared, gazing at him coolly.

"I promise I have not lied to you once, Sam. I wouldn't do that."

"Okay, but I'm sure you can understand my caution. I hardly know you. We've only just met."

"I know, sweetness, and if I do anything at all that you don't like, you just come right out and tell me. Okay?" he asked. "That goes for Justin and Chet, too."

"All right," she answered on a sigh.

"Do you need any help packing your things?"

"No, thanks anyway, but I prefer to do it myself." She began to do just that.

"Justin, Chet, there's been another change of plans," Roan said through his and his brothers' intimate mind link. *"Sam is going to come and stay in our spare room. I'll explain later, but I don't want her to be alone. From now on one of us will be with her at all times. I think whoever she's running from has found her."*

"Fuck! I'm glad you were able to convince her to come home with us, where she'll be safe. I'll contact Jonah and let him know we are bringing our human mate home so the others will know not to let her see their wolf tendencies," Justin replied.

"Shit, how is she going to react to the unconventionality of the relationships between our Alphas and the Betas and their mates?" Chet asked with agitation.

"You don't have to worry on that score. I've already told her the men of our family like to share their women."

"How did she take that?" Justin inquired.

"Much better than I expected. Even though she may trust us, she is still wary, so make sure you don't do anything to upset her. I don't think it would take much to send her running," Roan cautioned.

"Okay, I'll try to curb my dominant tendencies, but you and I both know it won't be long before we try to get her into our beds," Justin said firmly.

"Yeah, I know. Just try and give her a few days to get to know us. Okay?"

"Yeah, I'll try, but I'm not promising. She wants us just as much as we want her. If she makes the first move, I'm not holding back."

Sam finished packing, and they walked back out to the parking lot and to her car. Roan was appalled at the condition of Sam's rusted bomb of a car but didn't feel it was right for him to comment just yet. He made sure to get a good look at the tires. Seeing they had plenty of tread, he sighed over the fact she had at least one thing safe on her car, but there was no way he could tell the condition of the brakes, and he wasn't about to let her drive that piece of junk without checking.

"Let's go and pick up Chet. He wanted to drive back with me, then we can come and get your car, sweetheart," he suggested in a light tone, not wanting her to know he had an ulterior motive.

"That's not necessary. I'll follow you to the club. You'll save on gas that way."

Her last statement and the condition of her car made him realize she was broke.

Oh, honey, you are in financial trouble as well, aren't you! Taking a deep breath, he knew he was going to have to relent. Thank goodness it was less than a mile to the club. He didn't want to have to explain his protectiveness toward her by clarifying he didn't want her driving that piece of shit.

"Okay, but when we get Chet, I want you to let him drive your car. These roads aren't familiar to you, and I don't want you getting lost. Are you ready, Sam?"

"Yes, lead the way," she replied. They both got into their cars and headed out of the parking lot.

Roan sighed with relief when he pulled up into a parking space outside the club. He'd already contacted his brothers through their link to tell them he wanted Chet driving her car. Once she was in a relationship with them, the first thing he planned to do was buy her a brand-new vehicle. He and his brothers were quite well off and didn't have to think before they spent any money. It came in handy, having a productive family that had great business acumen. They had invested money over the years, and those investments had proved very lucrative.

Chet was waiting for them on the pavement and headed toward Sam when she pulled up. Justin had gone on to the den ahead of them, intent on warning the pack members of their mate's arrival and also to make sure the spare room was ready for her. He watched as Sam scooted across the seat to let Chet take the wheel, put the car into reverse, and headed home.

* * * *

Samantha looked at Chet's profile as he drove her junk heap. She was embarrassed about the state of her car, but there was nothing she could do about it. All her money had gone into paying the bills and keeping a roof over her and Peter's heads, and then after she had left her home she'd had to work from hand to mouth.

Sighing, she turned away from Chet to stare out the side window. She was so tired of being alone and working just to survive. It would be so nice to have a cushion of money she could use for a rainy day, but she didn't see that happening anytime soon. Pulling her optimistic personality to the fore, she thought about how thankful she should be to have landed a job so quickly when she needed it. She was also on her way to the three Domain brothers' home. The first thing she was going to do was find out how much they were going to charge her for leasing a room with them, and then she intended to bathe and crawl into bed. It had been so long since she'd had a decent meal and a good night's sleep.

"You need new brake pads, darlin'. I can feel and hear metal grinding when I push on the pedal, and the steering's pulling to the left," Chet said.

"What I really need is a new car," Sam replied with a weary sigh.

"Well, don't worry about it now, Sam. Maybe I can have a look at your car for you," Chet suggested.

"Oh really? I would appreciate it if you could. I know my car isn't safe."

"You bet I will, darlin'. But since you'll be living and working with us, I think it would be wise if you got a lift into the club with one of us. Roan and I have the most shifts, and Justin just fills in occasionally."

"What else does Justin do?" she asked curiously.

"Oh, he helps our cousins Chris, Blayk, and James with the security business. Blayk is a doctor and doesn't really have much time to deal with that side of things anymore, so Justin is taking over from him."

"Oh, well it must be nice to have a medical practitioner in the family."

"You have no idea," Chet muttered.

Sam didn't think she was supposed to have heard that comment and didn't know what he meant by it, so she remained silent. Just as she was beginning to think her tired, burning eyes were going to close on her, Chet slowed the car and turned onto a driveway, in through great big wrought iron gates. She turned back and watched them close automatically. For a moment she felt trapped and had trouble taking a breath, but she threw off her paranoia and looked back to the front. The house that came into view took her breath away. It was so big and so beautiful. The image of large plantation houses with their white columns flashed through her mind. As gorgeous as it was, she felt as if she should ask Chet to turn her car around and take her back to town.

She didn't belong here. These people were obviously wealthy, and she didn't have two nickels to rub together. How the hell was she supposed to stay here when she couldn't afford anything but chain-store clothes and even then that was sometimes a stretch? Often she'd had to resort to shopping in the secondhand stores.

What the hell are you thinking, Sam? You should be demanding that he take you to the club.

But she didn't want to be alone anymore. She was sick and tired of being scared and lonely. These three men drew her like a magnet to metal, and even though she had no idea why, she was curious enough to find out.

Chapter Five

Chet had been watching Sam from the corner of his eye since the moment he had sat in the driver's seat of her car. She had been looking at him for about fifteen minutes, her expression going from soft and dreamy to frowning concern. He would have given anything to ask what was going through her pretty head but held off. Justin was pushy enough for all of them, and he didn't want her to feel as if she was cornered.

Slowing her car, he turned into the drive of the pack property and through the automatic gates, which thankfully Roan had left open. When Sam turned back after he drove through the gates and they got to the house, he saw awe pass across her face then what looked like fear. Parking the vehicle in Roan's designated spot, he got out and went around to Sam. She was still sitting frozen in the passenger seat, so he opened her door to help her out.

"Are you all right, darlin'?" he asked as he held his hand out to her.

"Yes," Sam replied, but her voice had risen to a higher pitch.

"You have nothing to be worried about, Sam. Everyone here will like you. Just relax, darlin'."

"I'll try."

He led her to the door of the massive carport, they stepped into the entry hall, and he guided her toward the kitchen dining room. Everyone was already seated at the long table, and food was just being served.

Justin got up from his seat, and so did Roan. Chet stood behind Sam and placed his hands on her shoulders while his brothers stood to either side of her.

"Everyone, I'd like you to meet Samantha Winters. She'll be staying with us for a while and also working at the club," Justin announced.

Chet looked down to see Sam had bowed her head, her eyes toward the floor. Little did she know that her submissive gesture would please his family but most of all his Alphas.

The Alphas shared responsibility in leading their pack, but if there was ever any conflict with decision making and Jonah, the lead Alpha, decided to take control, his word was Pack Law.

Chet was often amazed at the power of his Alphas but especially of Jonah. He could use his voice to command at will and demand acquiescence, as could Mikhail and Brock, but Jonah was the much more formidable of the three.

Everyone in the pack had responsibilities, and no one took their tasks lightly. There was a chain of command that had to be obeyed, even though all pack members were an integral part of the family and had input into what decisions were made.

Roan, Justin, and Chet had planned to be Betas since they had reached puberty. Most of the time pack members were born into the levels of hierarchy, but sometimes, if a wolf proved he was worthy, he could work his way up the ranks. Chet and his brothers were now one step away from reaching their goal. They only had to prove to the Alphas they had the strength needed to keep the pack safe.

But how the hell they were going to do that when they hadn't been challenged by the other Betas, or by anyone else, he had no clue.

"Come on, honey, and I'll introduce you around." Justin took hold of Sam's hand. He led her over to Jonah, Mikhail, Brock, and Michelle.

Once the introductions were over, Justin seated her next to him, and Roan sat at her other side. Damn, he was going to have to work out a system with Roan about taking turns with the seating arrangements. He knew Justin wouldn't relinquish his seat as he considered himself the most Alpha out of the three of them.

Angie, their chief cook and housekeeper, and her daughter Cindy greeted Sam, and Michelle, along with Keira and Talia, tried to put her at ease. But he could tell she was uncomfortable. Chet wished he knew what he could do to get her to relax, but nothing came to mind. Taking the chair next to Roan, he began to eat.

"How can you still be hungry?" Sam asked Roan quietly. "You just ate dinner at the club."

"We have fast metabolisms, darlin'. We eat a lot," Chet replied, leaning forward to see her around Roan, giving a smile and a wink. "You should eat something, Sam. You hardly touched your dinner."

"Thank you, but I'm just not hungry."

With dinner over, he glanced at Sam and saw she was barely able to keep her eyes open, so he stood and walked up behind her.

"Do you want to go to your room now, darlin'? You look exhausted," he whispered quietly against her ear. At her nod he pulled her chair back and helped her to her feet. His poor little darlin' was so tired she barely glanced around as he led her to the third floor, where their rooms were. He showed her to her room and where the bathroom was and left her to bathe while he went to get her bags from her car.

His brothers were already in their living room when he returned. Justin was pacing back and forth in agitation and Roan was sprawled out on the sofa, looking relaxed, but he knew better. They were both wound tighter than a clock spring. His wolf, hearing water splashing in the bathroom, began chafing at the bit to be set free. Imagining Sam in their tub, gloriously naked, made his dick jerk against the zipper of his jeans. Now he understood what had his brothers all fired up. Hearing a moan and another splash, he ground his teeth and adjusted his throbbing dick.

Justin turned to him with a scowl. "Get her to hurry the hell up before I go in there, haul her out, and jump her bones."

"Maybe you should go for a run." Chet cursed the low, gravelly tone of his voice as his wolf made its presence known, his control hanging by a thread.

"Let's go," Justin growled. He and Roan headed toward the door.

Chet should have been going with his brothers to release some of the sexual tension they felt at having their mate in their home, but he didn't want to leave her alone for a second.

Justin and Roan slammed the door behind them without a backward glance, and he was truly thankful they left when they did, because less than a second later the door to the bathroom opened.

The sweet scent of oranges, peaches, and vanilla drifted to his nostrils along with the aroma of his sexy little mate. He looked up as her head appeared around the corner of the hall.

"Could you please bring my bags to my room so I can get dressed?" Sam asked.

Chet wondered if she had anything covering her and, without thinking about his actions, picked up her bags and stalked toward her. Sam's eyes widened, and he heard her gasp as she ducked back out of sight. Picking up his pace, he followed her to the bathroom door and dropped her bags to the floor. There she was, standing uncertainly, her face flushed and clean from her bath, wrapped in his robe. Inhaling, he growled when her scent mixed with his assailed his olfactory senses. As if in a dream he reached out and snagged her around the waist and drew her up against his body. Her waist was so tiny he thought he may be able to wrap her with his arm.

She tilted her neck, and he could tell by the angle she would end up hurting her muscles, so he pulled his arm free and grasped her hips in both his hands. He cursed the fact that he could feel her hip bones jutting into his flesh even through the bulk of his robe. He lifted her until she was on eye level with him and dropped his gaze to her lush lips, hankering for a taste. Placing her hands on his shoulders to steady herself, she licked those cupid bows and glanced up again.

"What are you doing?" she asked breathlessly.

Knowing damn well she knew what he wanted, he didn't answer. Instead he slowly lowered his head until their lips were a scant inch apart. When she didn't protest but lowered her eyes to his lips, he groaned and moved forward until their lips met.

Not moving for a brief moment, Chet savored the first contact of her mouth to his, then, growling, he brushed his flesh over hers in soft, slow passes so she could become acquainted with his touch. Again, when she didn't protest or pull away, he deepened the kiss.

He opened his mouth and licked her lips with his tongue. Her soft moan made his balls ache and his cock throb. Pushing his way into her mouth, he tasted every inch of her sweetness. She wrapped her arms around his neck and her legs around his waist, which only made it harder for him to control his wolf and his raging desire. Her warm, wet pussy was now against his crotch with only the material of his jeans as a barricade, and the heat of her seared his cock. She whimpered into his mouth as he moved his hand from her ribs down under the robe to her ass. Kneading her fleshy globes, he thrust his cock against her wet, fragrant pussy as their mouths stayed connected and their tongues fought for supremacy.

The sweet aroma of her desire called to him and his wolf. He had never smelled anything so delectable in his life. Wrapping his tongue around hers, he drew it into his mouth and suckled on her like he imagined her doing to his cock, making his wolf howl. Moving a couple of steps, he planted her back against the wall in the hall and pinned her with his body. Easing an arm beneath her ass, he slowly untied the robe, spreading the material aside so he had access to her naked flesh. Growling into her mouth when she withdrew her tongue and finally her mouth from his, he rested his forehead against hers and opened his eyes and nearly came in his pants.

Her irises were nearly hidden by her largely dilated pupils and were glazed over with lust. Following the pink in her cheeks he looked down her neck and chest. She was absolutely exquisite. He knew she would be, but his imagination hadn't done her justice. Hard brown-and-rosy nipples stood out on her breasts, which were creamy white, the delicate blue veins visible under her skin, and her mounds were a delectable handful.

Chet moved his hand up and cupped her warm, soft flesh, groaning with delighted arousal as her turgid peak stabbed into the palm of his hand. His mouth salivating for a taste, he kneaded her breast and slowly lowered his head. Her citrusy scent wrapped around him, and he opened his mouth, sucking the hard tip in between his lips, and he knew in that moment that one taste of his mate would never be enough.

He let her flesh go, moving his hand away, but kept suckling on her sensitive nub and smoothed his hand down over her belly. She bucked her hips into his and mewled when he thrust his forward. His jeans were becoming damp from the juices leaking out of her cunt, and he needed to feel her slick heat against his fingers. Moving his palm down over her stomach, he caressed his way around her thigh, touching her soft, wet labia with the tips of his fingers. She was so hot and wet and her scent was calling so strongly to his wolf, he could barely restrain his animal from taking over and claiming her right then and there.

Knowing he had to get control, he threw his head back, closed his eyes, and inhaled deeply. His wolf was on the precipice of taking over. He felt claws erupt on the hand under her ass and quickly withdrew his fingers from against her wet pussy. He looked down. Seeing her eyes widen with shock, he knew his eyes had changed to gold. Releasing her, he let her slide down his body, and when she was steady on her feet, he stepped back and turned away as she clutched the gaping robe.

"What the hell are you?" she whispered through ragged pants for air.

"Sam," he growled. "Go to your room, darlin', and lock the door."

Listening intently he heard the rustle of her robe as she closed it, and then she ran, the door to the bedroom slammed closed, and his wolf's senses picked up the slight snick as the lock was engaged.

"Roan, Justin, I just fucked up in a big way." He ran for the door to their suite. Pulling his clothes from his body, he ran down the stairs and out into the cool night air. Bones popping and cracking, muscles contorting, he leapt from the front steps with two legs and landed agilely on four. He ran through the trees, leaped over fallen limbs, and howled.

"What did you do?" Justin asked.

"I kissed her and nearly lost control of my wolf. My hands began to change, and she saw my eyes. I had to tell her to go to her room and lock the door. I was so fucking close to biting her, claiming her, I had to get out of there."

Chet could smell that his brothers were close. Leaping a fallen tree, he came upon them suddenly in a clearing. The moonlight shone on their glossy pelts. Roan's wolf stepped forward, his golden eyes on Chet.

"Fuck, Chet. You were the one to tell us to leave, and here you are telling us you nearly claimed her. What the hell? Was she scared?" Roan inquired.

Chet licked his muzzle sheepishly. *"Yeah, sort of."*

"What the fuck does that mean?"

"She was more nervous than scared, but she did what I told her." Justin began to pace the clearing, aggravated, but Chet continued, *"We're going to have to tell her what we are. Sam needs to know the truth about us so she doesn't become frightened and take it into her head to run off."*

"I think we should leave it until morning, unless she comes out of her room again tonight. But after what you just told us I don't think she will. Let her get a good night's rest, and we'll deal with this first thing. It would be better if one of the other women were around when

we tell her. Their presence will help keep her calm while we answer all her questions," Justin explained.

"Okay. I'm sorry. If I had realized how hard it would be to control my wolf after I got my first taste of her, I would never have laid a hand on her. I've never felt anything like it before. All I could think about was burying my cock into her wet, creamy pussy and claiming her. Nothing else mattered. I don't think I would have cared if the room had been full of people. My wolf got away from me." Chet looked to each of his brothers. "I don't know how much longer I can be around her and not stake a claim."

Justin woofed softly in acknowledgement, but his instructions were stern. "You're gonna have to keep your distance. No touching or kissing unless she makes the first move. But only after she knows what we are. It's not fair to Sam. She should know all the facts before we try to talk her into staying with us and being our mate."

Justin leapt lightly atop the fallen tree and looked back at Chet and Roan. Narrowing his eyes on Chet, he ordered, "Don't come back until you've got your wolf under control. The last thing we need is for you to break down her door and claim her without her consent."

"I wouldn't do that, Justin." Chet felt his lips lifting, baring his teeth in annoyance. "Fuck, why do you think I told her to go to her room and ran outside?"

Justin bounded down the other side of the log. Roan cleared it in a flying leap that sprayed dead leaves behind his back paws. Though out of sight, Justin's answer came to Chet loud and clear.

"Because I had to do the same thing, and so did Roan, and we haven't even kissed her yet!"

Chapter Six

Sam leaned back against the door and groaned quietly. What the hell had she been doing? The image of Chet looking at her breasts just before he sucked a nipple into his mouth heated her face with unparalleled desire. She couldn't believe she had let the man kiss her and nearly fuck her up against a wall, for God's sake.

When she had looked up into his eyes they had been a glowing gold color. The sight had awed her and also made her more than a little nervous. She'd never seen anything like it before. When he had growled at her to lock herself in her room, she had been too dumbfounded to question him. Easing away from the door, she moved to the bed, removed the robe, and slid between the sheets. It was going to be a long night.

Just as her head settled on the pillow, she flinched at the sound of a wolf howling into the night. That sound made her heart clench. It was so full of sadness and loneliness, she wanted to get dressed, go outside, and comfort the animal.

Get a grip, Sam. The only thing you would get if you could even find the wolf is dead. He would eat you for his dinner.

Pushing her whimsical thoughts aside, she sighed and closed her eyes. She hoped the man who had been watching her from the car hadn't been Gerard Long. It was probably just a coincidence, but she'd been too nervous to take any chances. Maybe he had lost her trail or finally come to realize that she really wasn't interested in him. That man scared her more than Peter had, and that was saying something.

Sadness engulfed her as she thought of the child she had lost. Even though she had only carried her baby for two months, grief would still rear its ugly head and swamp her from time to time. She'd hardly had any time over the last six months to think of her loss, but being around the three Domain brothers made her dream the impossible. Her thoughts were so convoluted she didn't know where her own mind was. She pictured herself cradling a baby against her chest while she fed it and the three sexy brothers watched her. The image was so real in her mind that she could smell their unique scents and nearly feel the weight of her child against her skin.

Tightness took hold of her chest, and tears tracked down her cheeks. Pain wracked her as she thought of the baby she had lost and would never be able to hold, love, or nurture. She hadn't even known whether her fetus was a boy or a girl. Pushing a fist against her mouth to stifle her sobs, she cried for her loss. The loss of never being able to hold her baby in her arms or to smell the sweet scent of her child or to have the opportunity to guide him or her into adulthood. She would never know the joy of looking into her baby's face, seeing it smile at her with the unconditional love only a child could give.

Burying her face into her pillow, she sobbed, great wracking sounds of grief. She'd really only cried once, and that was the day she had lost her beloved child. Trying to keep a roof over her head and then holding off Peter's friends and colleagues had taken all her concentration. But for some reason, being with these men brought it all to the forefront of her mind, and she couldn't hold her emotions in another moment. She cried and cried and cried, oblivious to her surroundings.

She heard a faint click but was too caught up in her own grief to take much notice. Warmth penetrated her skin as hands lifted her and then surrounded her. She was pulled into comforting arms. When the tears finally slowed and the pain receded slightly, she became aware of the fact that she was totally naked in the arms of the three Domain brothers. She hid her face against Justin's chest, knowing how ravaged she looked after such a crying jag, but sighed with contentment at being surrounded by all three men. She was sitting sideways on Justin's lap with Roan at her back and Chet close to her front. Chet was looking at her with such worried concern as he rubbed a hand up and down her arm in soothing strokes. Roan was rubbing her back while Justin was stroking her hair.

"Shh, it's okay, little one, everything will be all right," Justin murmured.

Sam was only spasmodically hiccupping now but was thankful for the reassurance these three men offered her. Roan reached out and took her chin gently into his hand, tilting her head up and away from her protective haven.

"Do you want to talk about it, sweetness?"

"N–Not yet," Sam replied in a voice husky with tears.

"Why don't we all go to the kitchen and get a drink?" suggested Justin.

"O–Okay."

"Here, let me help you with your robe, darlin'." Chet began to put it around her body with Roan and Justin's help.

"It's your robe." She inhaled his masculine scent.

"Yeah, but it looks so much better on you, darlin'." She looked up to see him smiling down at her.

When she was covered with the sleeves rolled back so she could see her hands, Sam smiled at the three men. She was about to follow Roan to the door, but Justin scooped her up into his arms and carried her.

"I can walk, you know."

"I know you can, honey, but I love the way you feel in my arms." Justin smiled down at her.

"What do you want to drink, darlin'?" Chet asked as Justin sat down at the kitchen table with Sam seated across his thighs.

"Tea, please."

"Lean back and relax, Sam." Justin helped her get comfortable so he could support her back with his arm and shoulder. Roan sat down across from her, and when Chet had finished making the drinks, coffee for them and tea for her, he sat on the chair next to them.

They sat in companionable silence until she had drunk half her tea, and then Justin spoke.

"Talk to us, honey. Tell us why you are so sad."

Sam couldn't keep quiet anymore. She needed to purge what she had kept bottled up inside so it wouldn't destroy her, so she began talking.

"I married young, at the tender age of eighteen, and had planned to go to culinary school, but that never happened. My husband didn't want to waste money on me, so I put my plans on the back burner.

"Peter Strom, my husband, had opened his own insurance business, and we needed money to live until he was established. So I worked at whatever I could to pay the rent.

"I was so in love with him, or thought I was, that I would have done anything to support him. We were happy for the first twelve months, or seemed to be, and he worked hard trying to make a success of his business. Then he began to turn spiteful." Sam paused and finished off her tea. She looked to Roan and Chet, and they looked at her encouragingly.

"Go on, honey," Justin said and stroked her hair.

"He never had anything nice to say to or about me, and since he was six years older than I was, I thought I was somehow lacking.

"He started picking on the way I dressed, the way I wore my hair, and the curves of my body. He used to tell me I was ugly and my boobs were too big. Little by little he chipped away at my self-esteem until I had nothing left inside but emptiness and bitterness toward the man who was supposed to love me.

"Peter started coming home late every night, and when I questioned him he became so furious with me, I backed off and tried to soothe him instead. In the end I was glad he didn't come home until the early hours of the morning, because I had become so afraid of his mood swings and temper that I was scared he would take it out on me." She took a deep breath and fidgeted with her mug.

"Do you want another tea, darlin'?" Roan asked.

"Please." She handed over her empty mug and clutched her now-empty hands. Following Roan with her eyes, she continued.

"When he was home he would criticize everything about me, even what I cooked him for dinner. Peter's business failed. He found another job with a large insurance company, and I thought he would be happier without the worry of the business hanging over his head. Ha, what a joke. Even though he had a job, he stopped contributing to the running of the household, and I had to take on a second job just to make ends meet.

"One day six months ago, he arrived home before me. I was two months pregnant, but I still had worked for eight hours at the local supermarket ringing up groceries and then worked another six hours in a bar serving drinks. My feet and back were aching, and I was so tired I could barely keep her eyes open. I knew as soon as I opened the door that Peter was home. Feeling the thick tension in the air, I headed straight for the kitchen, trying to avoid him. Just as I finished my glass of water, I knew he was there, standing behind me. The hair at my nape stood on end." Sam paused, reached out for the mug of fresh tea Roan handed her, and sipped.

"Thanks," she said and took a deep breath. Her body was tense, and each of the men with her offered her comfort in some small way. Justin was still stroking her hair and Roan reached for her free hand and enveloped it in his, while Chet sat close and rubbed her shoulder.

"He grabbed me by the hair and dragged me into our bedroom, causing me to cry out with pain and fear. Pushing at him to get him to release me was utterly futile and only further exacerbated his rage. He cursed me and threw me at the bed, and when I tried to scramble away from him, he pinned me in place. Then the accusations began.

"He accused me of having an affair, of running around behind his back, spreading my legs for every male in the city. If the notion hadn't been so ludicrous, I would have laughed. When was I supposed to have found the time or energy to go cavorting around with other men when I worked two jobs? And I realized after a moment I had actually asked that question out loud.

"Peter didn't reply. Instead he started hitting me. He cursed me for holding him back and told me he hated my guts. He was smart about his abuse. He didn't hit my face where any of the bruises could be seen. It didn't matter anyway, because I didn't leave our home for three days. After punching me in the stomach and chest, he packed up his belongings and then left the apartment without a backward glance or care for my condition." Her breath hitched on a sob, and she closed her eyes for a moment to regain control.

"We're with you, honey. You're all right now," Justin said quietly and rubbed her back.

"It took me thirty minutes to make my way into the bathroom, and I stood under the warm water in the shower crying my eyes out as I lost my newly formed baby. I collapsed to the floor with such agony and grief. How long I spent sitting on the floor of the shower I have no idea. I only remember the cold water finally penetrating my pain-filled heart and body, and I literally crawled from the cubicle. I existed in a catatonic state of grief and pain for days on end, but I finally came to terms with my loss, pulled myself together, and began to live again."

Roan moved from his chair and began to pace the kitchen. She couldn't see his eyes as his head was lowered, but she could see the muscle in his jaw ticking, and his fists were clenched.

Chet's body had hardened with tension, and he was gripping the edge of the table with his fingers so hard that his knuckles were white. She wasn't prepared to look at Justin but wondered why they were so angry. She was the one who had been abused and lost her baby, not them.

"I know I should have gone to seek medical help, but I was so humiliated at what my husband did to me, I didn't see anyone. It took me three days to be able to move without hunching over, and by that time I had lost both my jobs.

"I eventually sought out medical attention and was told I was lucky that my reproductive organs hadn't been affected by the attack. Of course I told my doctor I had been mugged, since I didn't want to see sympathy or pity in those kind eyes.

"Peter sent me divorce papers and our divorce was finalized in quick succession. What I didn't realize was that my husband had spread the word amongst his seedy work colleagues at the large insurance company he worked for, saying that I would spread my legs for anyone.

"I found another job and was working in a small café, barely earning enough to pay the rent, and the door knocking started. I was so scared to find strange men standing outside my apartment door leering at me until I slammed the door closed in their faces. After questioning one man about why he was at my door, he apologized for harassing me and he told me what Peter had done.

"Most of the men must have received the message, because in the end I just didn't bother to answer the door at all. But there was one man who kept persisting, and I was scared by the cold, evil look in his eyes. He introduced himself as Gerard Long, and every week after that, without fail, he would pound on my door until I called the police on him. Things were quiet for a while, but then he started up again.

"Only this time he somehow managed to get ahold of my phone number and used to whisper all the nasty things he wanted to do to me through the phone. He was such a sick individual and he scared me so much that I packed up my stuff, ended the lease on the apartment, and left town.

"I worked from town to town, state to state, until I arrived in Aztec," she stated emotionlessly and took a deep breath. Now that she was finally finished, she was totally exhausted and emotionally drained. Her eyelids were too heavy to keep open, and she snuggled into Justin and gave up the fight.

* * * *

"Fuck. Our little mate has been to hell and back," Justin said quietly, careful not to wake his precious bundle. He rubbed his cheek over the top of her head and inhaled her exquisite citrus-peach scent.

"If I ever get my hands on her ex, I'm going to rip him apart," Roan said in a deep growl.

"I can't believe…Why…? Fuck!" Chet exclaimed in anger.

"I don't know. But we have to protect her. One of us is to be with her at all times," Justin commanded. "I don't care how much she argues, she isn't to be left alone."

"Do you think the guy who was watching her at the motel is the one who's stalking her?"

"We won't know for sure until we run a check on Gerard, which we'll do first thing in the morning. For now I think we should get out mate into bed. She needs to rest. She's so tired she has dark smudges under her eyes."

"You're right. Let's take her to my room. At least with her cuddled up between us we'll know if she has nightmares or doesn't sleep through the night. Besides, I want her next to me," Justin explained as he rose to his feet and carried her to his room, careful not to jostle Sam too much and wake her.

He gently placed her in the middle of his large bed, and his brothers helped him get the robe off her, and then he slid in beside her. Roan got in on her other side, and Chet lay across the bottom of the mattress.

"Tomorrow night I get to sleep where you are, Roan," Chet said firmly.

"Only if Sam doesn't put up a fuss over sleeping with us," Roan replied quietly.

"I won't," Sam whispered and rolled over into Justin's embrace. "I feel safe here."

Justin smiled and looked down at Sam. She had her head resting on his shoulder and her arm over his chest. As she slid back into sleep, her breathing deepened and evened out once more. Roan moved up close to her back until he was spooning her. Chet was probably touching one of her legs or feet. It was a wolf trait to want to be touching the people they loved, especially their mate.

She was such a tiny little thing compared to him and his brothers, but she felt so right being here, in his arms. She trusted them. That was a good start. He just hoped after they told her what they were she would still feel the same way about them.

* * * *

Sam was fighting against waking. She was so warm and content she didn't want to surface to face another day. Shifting her legs, she froze when they connected with hard bodies. Sighing, she remembered Justin had placed her into his bed and Roan and Chet had got in as well. No wonder she was so hot. She was surrounded by three tall, muscular, handsome men. She didn't want to wake up, because reality would then intrude and she would have to get up.

Today was her first day to start work at the Aztec Club, and even though she looked forward to earning money and being financially independent again, she was too comfortable to want to move.

"Morning, honey." Justin's deep cadence broke the silence. "How are you feeling?"

Sam lifted her head and squinted through sleep-heavy lids, her gaze connecting with his.

"I'm good."

"Glad to hear it, sweetness. Do you want some coffee?" Roan asked from behind her and nuzzled her neck.

"That would be nice."

"Why don't you go take a shower, darlin', and by the time you're done the coffee should be ready," Chet suggested.

"Hmm-mmm, sounds good."

"What do you usually have for breakfast, honey?"

"Just coffee."

"Well, that's going to change starting now," Justin stated firmly. "You need to start your day off right, honey. Come on, up and at 'em, daylight's burning."

"Okay," Sam replied and shivered when the covers were pulled away from her body. *Shit! I'm naked, when did that happen?* Then she remembered her crying jag and telling these three men about how she had ended up in Aztec. She had fallen asleep on Justin, and he had carried her to his bed. He must have removed her robe so she would sleep more comfortably.

"God, you're sexy, darlin'," Chet said in a deep, gravelly voice.

"Uh, thanks." She felt her cheeks heat.

"You don't need to be embarrassed, sweetheart. Your little body is beautiful and perfect," Roan rasped.

"Go on, honey. Go and get your shower," Justin suggested and helped her up.

Sam snatched the robe from the floor and quickly covered her body, suddenly feeling very shy. She didn't care that her hands were hidden in the folds of material as she left for the bathroom. What worried her the most was that she could smell her own arousal. God, she hoped they couldn't scent how much she wanted them.

Chapter Seven

"I think we should tell Sam after breakfast," Roan said as he pulled the bacon from the grill. "Have Michelle on standby in case we need her help."

"I've already contacted Jonah, and he has Michelle, Keira, and Talia ready to step in if need be," Justin replied.

"Good," Chet said. "Fuck, I can't believe how nervous I am. I know we need to let her know what we are, but I'm so fucking worried about how she's going to react."

"React about what?" Sam asked as she entered the room.

"Hi, sweetness, you're just in time for breakfast. Sit down and we can all eat." Roan began to take the plates over to the table.

After breakfast was done, Sam got up to clear the table, but Roan halted her by placing his hand around her wrist.

"Sit down, sweetness, we need to talk."

"Have I done something wrong?" Sam asked Roan with a worried expression.

"No, Sam. We just need to explain a few things to you. Do you want more coffee?" He put off the inevitable for a moment.

Roan sighed when she shook her head. Taking a deep breath, he let it out slowly and glanced at his brothers. They were watching their mate intently.

"You know how you saw first Justin's and then Chet's eyes change to gold? Well, there is a reason for that, Sam. We're werewolves, sweetness, and you are our mate."

Roan observed Sam intently and saw her eyes widen and her pupils dilate. He sniffed the air and scented her nervousness.

Emotions, ranging from awe to fear and then disbelief, flitted across her face. She rose from her chair and backed away.

"W–What?"

"Honey, please don't be scared of us. We would never do anything to hurt you. Have we given you any reason to be afraid of us?" Justin asked.

"N–No." Sam gulped loud enough for Roan to hear.

"Sweetness, we will protect you with our own lives. Please don't back away from us," Roan appealed to her and held his hand out in a placating gesture.

"B–But there's no such things as w–werewolves."

"Darlin', we are living proof that there are. Come and sit down, Sam. You know we wouldn't hurt you. Please don't let the fact that we are a little more than human alter the way you look at us," Chet said and moved toward her.

When she didn't try and back away again Roan let out the breath he didn't know he'd been holding and his taut muscles relaxed slightly. He walked to her side and took her elbow, then guided her back to her seat.

"What do you mean I'm your mate?" Sam asked. "Wait, is everyone in this house a werewolf?"

"Yes, they are, honey. We are all related. Since we work together and it's a trait of our species, we like being close to the ones we care about. You are our mate, Sam. We knew it the moment we met you."

"But how could you know that, and what do you mean by *our* mate? Do you mean I'm mate to all three of you?"

"Honey, a mate is the human equivalent of a wife. You are meant to be a wife to all of us."

"How is that even possible? You want me to mate with the three of you? I'd never even heard of such a thing until you introduced me to your cousins and their wives. How does that even work?"

"Shh, darlin', it's okay. Don't panic. We won't do anything unless you allow us to," Chet said quietly.

"How do you know I'm your mate?"

"I knew the moment I caught your scent, sweetness," Roan explained. "It was so delectably exquisite I had the urge to change into my wolf form and roll around in it. Once I smelled you I just knew you were meant to be ours. We are drawn to you physically as well as emotionally. All three of us just want to wrap ourselves in your body and in the comfort of your arms and your heart. But I know it's way too soon for you, sweetness, so we will give you all the time you need to get used to us. If you decide to accept us as your mates, we will make love with you and bite into your flesh to claim you. The claiming bite won't cause you any pain, Sam. You will only feel pleasure at our touch."

"If I did agree and let you claim me, would you have to make love to me at the same time? And if so, how is that even possible?"

"We don't have to claim you together, honey," Justin clarified. "We can do it separately, but if we ever made love to you together, one of us would take your sweet pussy, the other would love your pretty ass, and one of us would fuck your mouth."

Roan could see thoughts flitting across her face and wanted to keep reassuring his mate that she had nothing to worry about from him or his brothers, but he waited patiently while she processed the information.

"How does biting me claim me?" she asked.

"When we claim you our DNA enters your body and then you belong to us. Your senses will be much better when we mark you. Your hearing, sight, and smell will be more enhanced," Chet answered.

"So it will change me?"

"Yes, honey. You won't turn into a werewolf, but your senses will be like ours. Our strength is greater and our senses sharper. We should also be able to communicate with you telepathically over time, once we have claimed you," Justin expounded.

"Can you do that now?" Sam asked, and Roan could hear the awe in her voice. "I mean, telepathy? With each other?"

"Yes, we can, darlin'. We have our own private link we use to communicate with each other and another common pack link we use to communicate with the rest of our family."

"Do–Does it hurt when you change?"

Roan accepted the change of subject and listened while his brother answered her.

"No, darlin'," Chet explained. "By the time you get to our age our bodies are used to the change. We only begin changing shape once we hit puberty. The first couple of shifts make our bones ache, but it's only similar to growing pains. After that it becomes easy."

"Do you only go furry when it's a full moon?" Sam asked, and Roan could see the gleam of amusement in her eye.

"No, sweetness, we can change whenever we wish to. The moon seems to pull at us more when it's full, but we don't have to change if we don't want to." Roan gave her a wink and smile.

"Are all the women werewolves, too?"

"No, darlin'," Chet replied. "There are only five women in the entire world who are shifters, and four of those were born with the werewolf gene."

"So, who wasn't?"

"Who wasn't what, honey?"

"Who wasn't born with the wolf gene, and why can she shift if she wasn't born a *were*?"

"Keira was shot, sweetness, and the only way to save her life was to change her. We don't go around changing humans. The process is agonizing and too violent. Keira was lucky she managed to survive the change," Roan explained.

"So how is the change done?"

"Honey, I don't think you want to know that."

"Yes, I do. I wouldn't have asked if I didn't."

Roan took her hand into his, and Justin leaned forward to take her other hand.

"Sam, the change is made by ripping into the stomach and organs. The wolf has to go deep, so DNA from the *were* can travel and take root in the tissue and blood of the human. It's not very often that they survive, so we don't change human beings unless it can't be avoided, as was the way in Keira's case," Justin clarified.

"Oh, my God. That's horrible. Poor Keira, she must have suffered so much."

"No, she didn't suffer from the change, sweetness. Keira was already unconscious and slipping away from her mates. The gunshots she sustained were lethal, Sam. It was the only way to save her life," Roan explained.

"You don't have many women in this house. How come?"

"We think that even in the womb, male traits are so dominant that they overpower female ones. Blayk, one of Talia's mates, is a doctor, and he has been looking into the science of werewolf conception. It seems that his suspicions of male domination have been confirmed. We don't know how to circumvent this phenomenon yet, but knowing Blayk, he won't give up until he finds a solution," Chet answered.

"So if you're all dominant, who's the boss?"

"Jonah is the most dominant and senior Alpha of the pack, but Mikhail and Brock rule alongside him with Michelle," Roan said.

"Oh that explains it."

"What does, honey?" Justin asked.

"When I first met Jonah and his brothers I felt intimidated by them, but especially Jonah. They all have this aura of power surrounding them," Sam explained.

"Yeah, they do, but Jonah has more dominance in his little finger than anyone else in the pack. If he decides to put his foot down, he can use his voice to get you to bend to his will. Mikhail and Brock can do the same, but when Jonah has his mind set on something then he rules. His final word is Pack Law."

"Everything you're telling me seems so surreal. I mean, I believe you, but I don't think I will fully understand or believe werewolves exist unless you show me. So, which one of you is going to show me your wolf?"

"Come here, sweetness." Roan gently tugged Sam onto his lap then watched as Justin and Chet stood and moved back a few paces. He didn't take his eyes from his mate while his brothers stripped out of their clothes. He nearly groaned out loud when she gasped and he smelled her leaking pussy. Their little mate was turned on by the sight of his naked brothers, and that gave him hope.

Hope that she trusted them enough to become aroused even after what they had just told her. She didn't try to get off his lap. Instead she wrapped an arm around his neck and stared at his brothers.

He could see the tip of her pink tongue peeking out from between her lips and wanted to bend his head to take a taste of her, but he held back. This was an awesome moment for their mate, and he wanted to see every nuance and expression which flitted over her features.

The sound of bones popping permeated the air, and Sam moved her free arm to cover her mouth with her hand. At first she looked horrified and then concerned, but when his brothers had finished changing forms she smiled. That smile lit up her whole face, and little dimples peeked out next to her lips.

"Oh, you're both so big. Can I pet?" she asked in her husky voice.

Roan finally slid his gaze from her face and watched as his brothers moved toward her in their wolf forms. Sam surprised him when she didn't hesitate. She withdrew the arm she had around his neck, and he stifled a growl as she moved on his lap, nudging his hard, throbbing cock. Then Sam sunk her fingers into his brothers' coats.

"Your fur is so soft. I thought it would feel much coarser." She whispered, but he heard her clearly.

His mate stood up and walked in between his brothers. She was so petite that their heads were on level with her chest. Turning toward him, she eyed him up and down and wrinkled her nose at him.

"I want to see you in your wolf form, too."

Roan got to his feet and moved away from the chair and began to undress, watching her the whole time. He saw her breath hitch in her throat and smelled her creaming pussy when he stood before her naked. Letting his human self fall away, he called to his wolf. Not once did he remove his gaze from hers, and when he was standing before her on four legs, he slowly moved closer. Hearing her laughter as she sunk her fingers into his coat was one of the best moments of his life. When she moved her fingers to behind his ears, he rumbled with contentment deep in his chest.

"You are all such gorgeous wolves. I can't believe I'm not having any trouble accepting this. I guess it comes from reading so much. I love to read about mythological creatures, and sometimes I find myself dreaming that they really do exist. The universe is so big, who knows, maybe aliens are real, too.

"God, listen to me ramble on. Why don't you change back? It's nearly time to head into work," Sam suggested.

First Justin then Chet changed back and began to dress. Roan had to really concentrate hard on pushing his wolf back. His animal was trying to dominate him by staying in wolf form, but he wasn't about to give in. Finally he re-dressed and watched the sway of Sam's hips as she left the room. As much as he loved and craved being near her, it was nice to be able to relax for a moment. Since the first time he had laid eyes on Sam, his wolf had been pushing to stake a claim.

"I don't know how much longer I can take this. My wolf nearly got away from me and took over. He was pushing to bite her here and now." Chet began pacing.

"We have to give her time to get used to us, Chet. We've only just told her what we are." Justin finished loading the dishwasher.

"I know that and you know that, but our wolves don't give a shit about any of it," Chet ground out. "They want her and don't care about the mechanics of things."

"If you don't calm down and control your wolf, I am going to make you stay home today," Justin commanded. "I don't care how much your beast is pushing, you will not do anything to jeopardize our chances with our mate."

Chapter Eight

It had been a long day, and Justin was tired. He and his brothers had conversed with their cousins and Alphas, Jonah, Mikhail, and Brock, about their investment properties and the security system, which had apparently just fried. He didn't like knowing the security around the pack grounds and house wasn't working, but they couldn't do anything about it until the next day at the earliest. Chris and Blayk had tried to work on the circuit boards to get the system up and running again, but it seemed their efforts had been futile. Even Greg, Jake, and Devon had taken a look, but they couldn't do anything either. It looked like they needed a whole new system.

After spending the morning working on the security system, he had spent the afternoon and night at the club. No matter where he was or what he was doing, Justin was going out of his mind with desire for their mate.

It had been four weeks since Sam had come to live with them, and still she hadn't said anything about letting them claim her. But since Sam was much more comfortable around him, his brothers, and their pack, if he had to wait another four weeks for her, then so be it. He would often find her in the living room on the sofa talking with Michelle, Keira, and Talia. The four women had become great friends.

While Sam was safe at the pack house, Justin still hadn't found anything on that guy, Gerard Long, who had been stalking his mate, and that frustrated him more than anything. There had been no other sightings of the man who had been watching Sam in the parking lot of the motel, and Justin wondered if the fucker had given up, whoever he was. Maybe it had just been a coincidence after all, like those bastards who had tried to feel Sam up in the back hallway that first night at the club.

He, Roan, and Chet made sure to touch and kiss Sam frequently, and she touched them in return. Some of her gestures had been downright provocative, and that gave him hope that she would eventually consent to mating with them. Whenever he pulled her close for a hug, she would give a little wiggle and rub up against him. She did it to his brothers as well, but he wasn't sure if she was aware of what she was doing. At night he would often sit with her on his lap, and again she would shift around until she was comfortable enough to settle down. But each time she moved, he had to clench his jaw to control his raging libido. His little mate's squirming caused his hard cock to pulse and leak pre-cum.

He ran in his wolf form every night and jacked off in the shower, just to keep control of his raging desire.

Tonight was no different. Now all he wanted to do was take a shower and crawl into bed with his mate. Sam had been sleeping with him and his brothers since the first night, and that didn't help his arousal problem. Even now he could smell her scent all over him, and his wolf was pacing restlessly beneath his skin.

Justin opened the bathroom door and froze midstride. Standing before him in all her naked glory was his mate. He perused her body from the top of her head down to the tips of her toes and inhaled deeply. His wolf pushed against him, trying to get free, but he pushed back, hard.

"Honey, you need to get out of here now. Go to the spare room and lock the door," Justin commanded in a deep, rumbling voice.

Instead of doing what he said, Sam walked up to him, stood on tiptoes, cupped the back of his neck with her hand, and pulled his head down. That action was all it took to break his control.

Justin growled and wrapped his arms around her delectable little body. He lifted her up until her crotch was aligned with his. He lowered his head and took her mouth. Thrusting his tongue between her lips, he tasted every nuance of flavor she had to give. No one woman had ever tasted as good as his mate. As soon as he had seen her, his cock had gone from its perpetual semihard to full-blown engorgement in less than a second, and now it was pulsing against the zipper of his jeans and his balls were aching. The urge to release his erection and bury himself in her hot, wet pussy was all he could think about.

Sliding his tongue along hers, he then flicked it upward and caressed the roof of her mouth. The little moaning and mewling sounds she made as he made love to her mouth fired his arousal even more. His wolf butted against him, urging him to claim her, and he knew if he didn't get control he would soon be in trouble. Slowing the kiss down, he finally withdrew his lips and rested his forehead against hers. Breathing heavily, he tried to regain his senses.

"Sam, I can't do this. If we continue on this path, I'm going to end up making love with you, and my wolf is pushing to claim you." He bent until she had her feet back on the floor. Then he released her and stepped away.

"I have thought about this long and hard," Sam whispered. "You and your brothers treat me with so much respect and have never raised your voices or hands to me. I trust you. All of you. I thought I was in love with my ex-husband, but it turns out that was just an infatuation. Peter claimed to love me, and he showed me just how much by abusing me. Not once have you claimed to love me, but you, Roan, and Chet have showed me with your actions that you care for me. I would like nothing better than to make love with you all and for you to claim me as your mate."

"Are you sure, honey?" Justin asked. "Once we start this we won't stop until you're ours."

"Yes, I'm very sure, and I don't want you to stop. I want this more than anything I have ever wanted before."

"I'm a dominant man, honey. I like to control what happens in the bedroom. Are you prepared to submit to me, to us?"

Sam nodded her head in affirmation.

"Then go and get into my bed. I am going to take a shower. We'll join you in a little bit."

Sam left to do his bidding immediately. His wolf was howling in his head with victory, and Justin knew if he didn't take the edge off his flaming libido he wouldn't last the night. He stepped into the shower, washed quickly, and then grabbed hold of his aching cock. He didn't need to fantasize too much since he had been on edge since the moment he woke and within moments was spewing cum against the tile wall.

Justin turned off the shower and toweled off quickly. He opened the link to his brothers. *"Roan, Chet, Sam has consented to mating with us. Meet me in my bedroom."*

The two howls that echoed in his head made him smile. Their patience was finally about to be rewarded.

* * * *

From the moment she had met the Domain brothers, Sam had been drawn to them. Little by little, both their actions and their words had shown her that they cared for her. She didn't know if what they felt for her was love, but hopefully that emotion would come in time.

She felt as if she somehow belonged here with these people, but especially Justin, Roan, and Chet. They took care of her, reminding her to eat when she forgot, holding her on their laps after a long day, and generally looking after her. Even if Sam didn't need them to look out for her, it was so nice to be able to lean on them and not have to face the world alone. The three men had come to mean a great deal to her, and slowly but surely they had worked their way into her heart until she couldn't bear to think of living without them.

She had spent the last three weeks observing the other women and their men, wondering how a relationship with more than one male worked. What she had seen had helped make up her mind. Michelle's, Keira's, and Talia's mates treated them like queens. The women were so happy and in love that Sam felt a little envious. All she ever wanted was to be loved for herself.

She had even tested her men by taunting them with her body, wiggling and squirming all over them, seeing how they would react. They had passed her tests with flying colors and hadn't put the moves on her without her consent. She had finally realized what she had been doing after kissing Justin earlier in the bathroom. His chivalrous actions had been the clincher. She didn't want to be without them in her life.

Now that she had decided to mate with them, Samantha was filled with excited energy and nervous arousal. She had been waiting for this moment for what seemed like so long, she couldn't sit still. Having done what Justin commanded, she was now in his bed, stark naked with the covers pulled up to her chin, but in a half-sitting, half-reclining position, leaning against the pillows resting on the headboard. She kept moving her legs and arms restlessly and clutching at the quilt. Her libido had been simmering for weeks, and now that the big moment was here, she was so turned on that she was scared she would climax from just one touch. The last thing she wanted to do was turn them off with her desperation. Never had she felt like this before, and she was also worried she wouldn't be able to reach an orgasm and satisfy their needs.

Groaning at her contradictory thoughts, she tried to settle her nerves down and breathed in and out a few times to control her rapid pants. It didn't seem to help. The only orgasms Sam had ever achieved had been self-induced. Peter had told her repeatedly that she was frigid and he didn't know why he bothered ever having sex with her, let alone marrying her. When he had reached for her in the darkness of the night, she had just lain beneath him passively and prayed the deed would be over quickly. He had never made sure she was ready for him, and she had often found sex painful. Even though she was nervous about making love with the three Domain brothers, she wasn't scared. She was more than ready to receive them into her body and in fact had been since the moment they had met. So she wasn't worried about pain.

Looking up when she heard movement near the bedroom door, her breath hitched in her throat at the sight which met her eyes. Justin, Chet, and Roan were making their way toward her, and they were gloriously naked.

Justin was tall, muscular but lean. His gray eyes pinned her with his hungry gaze, and she felt herself sinking into his depths. His muscles were toned and rippled as he shifted. His hard, long cock bobbed up and down. The head of his penis was an angry reddish purple in color, and he had a drop of clear fluid on the tip. She could see the striations of his muscles beneath his tanned skin, and that just made her hotter. He had an aura of dominance and power surrounding him that turned her on, and she couldn't wait to see how he would command her in bed.

Knowing she could trust them not to hurt her and to take care of her, she felt the last of her nervousness dissipate. As she stared at the three men, her lonely, empty heart filled with such emotion she had to struggle not to cry. Glancing away for a moment to get her emotions back under control, she looked up again.

Roan's brown pools glittered at her with such heat she felt the flames from where she lay in bed. He was bulkier than Justin and slightly shorter, and even though his stance was aggressive, with his hips jutting forward and his arms crossed over his chest, she knew he wasn't as intense as Justin. Although he could be just as dominant in his own way if the situation warranted it. She'd had a taste of their dominance just yesterday when she had gone outside the club for a breath of fresh air. Justin and Roan had come to find her and scolded her for putting herself in possible danger when she was supposedly being stalked. Justin had been too mad at her for not letting them know where she was, and Roan had been the one to lay down the law. He had told her she was to let them know where she was at all times, and if she wanted to go outside on her break, she was to take one of them with her. She had thought they were going over the top but, from the fierce look of determination in their eyes, had decided not to argue at that moment.

Roan took a step toward her and drew her eyes to his crotch. His cock wasn't as long as Justin's, but it looked thicker in the girth. It was also leaking out pre-cum, and she saw the way it pulsed with his heartbeat.

Licking her dry lips, she glanced over at Chet. He was just so damn big. If she didn't know he was the most lighthearted of the three, she would have been intimidated by his size. Bulging with muscles from his shoulders, biceps, and pecs to his washboard abs, slim hips, and large, sturdy thighs, he made her salivate with desire. And his cock was huge. It was as long as Justin's and slightly thicker than Roan's. She gulped with trepidation as Peter's small penis flitted through her mind. Quickly she pushed that image aside. There was no way she wanted him in her head at this very moment, and she felt a little guilty for the intrusion.

"Be very sure this is what you want, sweetness, because once we start I don't know if I'll be able to stop," Roan rasped.

"I'm sure, as long as you really want this, too."

"Why would you think we wouldn't, honey?" Justin inquired. "You are our mate, and we want to make love with you and claim you more than anything, right now. We have been on tenterhooks the whole time you have been living here and have dreamed about this moment."

She didn't really want to tell them of her worries because she knew her face would turn pink with embarrassment, but since these three men had been honest with her from the beginning, she could do no less. Taking a deep breath, she looked from one to the other and back to Justin again.

"I'm not very good at sex. My ex told me I was frigid," she explained quietly and quickly lowered her head.

"Look at me, Samantha," Justin commanded.

Tilting her head back until she was looking into Justin's gray eyes, she jutted her chin forward with false bravado.

"You are not in the least bit frigid, honey. If there was a problem with sex in your marriage, then it was all your ex-husband's fault. There is no way in hell that you are cold. Did he take the time to prepare you for his lovemaking?" Justin asked.

"No."

"There's your answer, sweetness. Foreplay is a big part of making love, and it is your partner's job to make sure your body is ready," Roan stated firmly.

They moved toward her at the same time. Justin climbed onto the bottom of the bed, and Roan and Chet got up on either side of her. Roan reached out and took her hands off the edge of the quilt and pushed it down, exposing her nakedness to their eyes.

"You are so perfect, honey." Justin smoothed his hands up and down her calves. "We are gonna love you so good."

She opened her mouth to respond but couldn't think of anything to say. Sam snapped her teeth closed. Just as Justin gently nudged her thighs apart, Roan cupped her cheek and turned her head his way.

He took her mouth at first with such gentle emotion, tears pricked the back of her eyes, and as he deepened the kiss she gave herself over to their gentle, loving touch. She moaned into Roan's mouth when Chet began to suckle on one of her nipples and Justin caressed her wet folds with the tips of his fingers.

"Fuck," Justin groaned. "You are so wet, honey, and you smell so fucking delicious. I have to have a taste."

Justin lapped at her pussy hole, which made her buck her hips up to push her vagina closer to his mouth. Moaning as he bestowed pleasure on her, Sam pushed her fingers through Roan's hair and pulled him in closer. She couldn't believe she had three men touching her all at once. The pleasurable sensations running through her were overwhelming.

Gasping for breath when Roan lifted his head, she looked down her body as Justin licked up through her folds and laved over her clit. Crying out on a sob of pleasure, she closed her eyes and arched her body.

"You taste so fucking good, honey. I love how your body leaks out more cream for me to lick up," Justin rumbled out against her slit.

Sam couldn't have answered even if she had wanted to. It seemed she had lost her voice along with her brain power. Her capacity to think coherently had floated away on a cloud of desire the moment they had begun to touch her.

As she turned her head and opened her eyes, Roan's throbbing dick caught her attention. It was so close that all she had to do was lean forward a little and lick. Unable to stop herself, she did just that.

The salty-sweet taste made her crave more of his essence. Opening wider, she took the head of his cock into her mouth and was rewarded by his groan. Laving the underside with her tongue, she set about pleasuring him in earnest and sucked him in farther.

"Fuck, sweetness, your mouth is heaven," Roan gasped.

Sam hollowed out her cheeks and sucked harder, pulling him into the back of her throat then easing back up, making sure to gently scrape her teeth over him.

"Fuck yeah," Roan rasped and gripped a handful of her hair.

Sam whimpered around her delectable mouthful when Chet sucked on a nipple while pinching the other between thumb and finger. Justin pushed a finger into her pussy and began a slow pump, all the while licking over her clit with rapid flicks of his tongue.

The muscles in her cunt clenched and released around Justin's digit, and he sped up his ministrations. She sobbed around Roan's cock and then cried out when Justin added another finger. Sam was so wet she could feel her juices leaking out of her pussy and down over her asshole. She had never felt anything like it. Her whole body was a mass of quivering desire and overwhelming need.

Justin wiggled his fingers around in her, and her hips shot up off the bed. God, if he kept that up she would come in minutes.

"It looks like you found her sweet spot, Justin," Chet rumbled out in a deep voice.

"Yeah," he growled against her pussy.

Tingles of warmth spread out over her as Justin caressed against that spot inside her again and again. She had no idea she had erogenous zones inside her pussy. Peter had never taken the time to learn her body, and even though she had brought herself to climax with clitoral stimulation, she had never had a toy or used her fingers inside to bring herself off.

Molten liquid lava traversed throughout her pussy, into her womb, her belly, and down her legs, making her toes curl. Pulling her mouth from Roan's cock, she gasped for breath as the internal muscles of her pussy began coil tighter. Arching her neck, she closed her eyes as her body bowed off the mattress. She was so close but couldn't seem to go over the edge.

Justin must have known what she needed, because he caged her clit gently between his teeth and sucked hard on her sensitive bundle of nerves. Sam screamed as her cunt clenched down on his embedded fingers, her body trembling as she climaxed hard. Stars formed before her closed lids, and she thought she was about to pass out from pleasure overload.

As her pussy contractions ebbed and finally diminished, and her breathing began to slow, she opened her eyes to find three sets of eyes staring at her hungrily.

"You are so fucking sexy when you come, honey," Justin rumbled. "I have to have you now."

Chapter Nine

Justin had never tasted ambrosia until he had tasted his mate's sweet cunt. Her flavor was a mix between sweet wine and salty brine, and one taste would never be enough. When he had sent her over into climax, he'd nearly followed her. She looked so beautiful when she came, he couldn't wait to send her over again, but this time he intended to be buried balls-deep inside her.

His wolf was just below the surface waiting to claim her, and he'd had a hell of a time seeing that she climaxed before he sunk his dick into her hot, wet pussy and bit into her flesh to make her his.

Sitting up between her thighs, he moved up closer to her, until his aching cock touched against her slippery folds. Placing his hands at her hips, he held her still and slowly began to forge his way inside her. The heat from her body wrapped around the crown of his dick, making him groan. Holding still when she whimpered and her pussy clenched around him, giving her time to adjust to his intrusion, he breathed in deeply, trying to control his urge to plunge into her hard and fast.

"Are you okay, honey?" he asked through panting breaths.

"Yes. God, you're so hard. I want more. Please?"

"I'll give you what you need, Sam. Just relax and let me do all the work," he rumbled in a deep voice. "You feel so fucking good, honey. I've never felt anything like it. This was meant to be, Sam. You're *mine!*"

Justin surged forward until his cock was touching her womb. Pushing his brothers aside, he covered her body with his and ravaged her mouth. Sweeping his tongue into her mouth, he tangled it with hers and began to thrust his hips, sliding his cock in and out of her sheath.

When his need for oxygen grew too great he lifted his head and looked down at Sam. Her eyes were glazed over with passion and her chest, neck, and cheeks were flushed pink. She looked so fucking sexy, his cock jerked inside her. Her cunt rippled around his dick, letting him know she was close to the edge, so while she was watching he let his wolf take some control. Canine teeth elongating in his mouth in preparation of claiming her, he watched her watch his eyes and knew they would be glowing gold. Just as her eyes rolled back in her head with pleasure when he thrust deeply, he bent down, licked her skin where shoulder and neck met, and sunk his teeth into her flesh.

She screamed out her climax as her blood filled his mouth. Her pussy contracted repeatedly around his dick, sending tingles of warmth shooting through his body. His balls drew tight to his body. He growled against her shoulder and then howled as he shot load after load of cum deep into her body.

When the last shudder left his body, he licked his claiming mark, knowing his healing saliva would close the bite immediately. Lifting his head, he looked down at his mate. Her eyes were closed, and she was still panting heavily. She opened her eyes and looked at him with such wonder that he felt joy and love fill his heart. He wanted to tell her he loved her but didn't want her thinking he was just saying it because of the sex, so he placed a gentle peck on her lips and eased out of her tight, clasping pussy. Then he moved off to the side and collapsed beside her.

He felt as weak as a newborn kitten with his shaking limbs, but he smiled with contentment. Only his mate could affect him so.

* * * *

Roan moved from beside Sam to give Justin room to flop down next to their mate. He couldn't wait to make love to her and claim her. From what he had seen as Justin fucked her, it was an incredible experience. His brother's legs still gave slight tremors as he lay beside her.

Now sitting between her splayed thighs, he leaned over her and kissed her deeply and passionately. Letting her feel all his love and the passion he felt for her, he blanketed her small body with his and aimed his cock for her pussy. She was so fucking wet and hot, he couldn't help but growl into her mouth as he pushed forward.

Heat enveloped his dick, and he groaned as her sheath clenched the head of his penis. He was thicker than Justin and didn't want to hurt Sam in any way. Being careful, he slowly began to push into her and groaned as her muscles and flesh parted and her sheath gloved him.

Holding still again, he waited for a signal from her that she was ready for more. He was only halfway inside her and wanted to go gently with her. Sam withdrew her mouth from his, gasping for breath. She reached out with her arms and tugged on his neck until his chest was touching her breasts. She wrapped her legs around his waist and pulled him in close with her strong leg muscles. He let her have her way just this once and followed her direction. He surged into her until the tip of his cock was as deep as he could get it, with his balls touching her ass.

Groaning with the exquisite sensations of finally being inside his mate, he withdrew carefully and then pushed back in. Using his arms, he braced himself again and watched her face as he began the erotic dance of advance and retreat. Increasing his rhythm incrementally, his hips thrusting, sliding his hard cock in and out of her wet heat, he let the exquisite friction build. When her breath became a sobbing cadence of his name in her sultry, husky voice, Roan lost it.

Pulling back, he forged his way into her sheath with hard, sharp, fast thrusts. He growled when she clenched around him, and he locked gazes with her. Her lips were open, and she was chanting his name as if it were a litany.

When he felt the warning tingle at the base of his spine he knew he was getting close to release. Bending to her neck and shoulder on the side opposite to where Justin had claimed her, he licked her skin, preparing her. Calling on his wolf, his eye teeth lengthened in his mouth and he bit down into her flesh. Howling against her flesh as she climaxed and bathed his cock in her cum, her scream of pleasure joining his, he let go of his control. His balls drew up in his scrotum, and then semen spewed up the length of his shaft and into his mate's pussy. His whole body quivered, feeling depleted as his strength left him. Sam's body continued to squeeze him with aftershocks and milked the last of his cum from his body.

Gently pulling his cock from her body, he ran his hands over her hips and stomach in a soothing gesture until her breathing went back to normal and her body stopped shaking. Placing a chaste kiss on her forehead, he flopped down on the other side of her and looked over at Chet. He began to get worried when he saw the feral gleam in his brother's eyes.

* * * *

Chet was so close to changing into his wolf, he was barely hanging on. Watching his two older brothers make love with her and bite her to bond them together had almost sent him over the edge of reason.

Crawling down the bed when Roan took his place beside Sam, he inhaled the scent of her cunt mixed with the seed from his brothers. He wanted to go slow and take things easy with her, but he didn't think his wolf was going to let him. Gripping her rib cage, he flipped her over onto her stomach.

"Hey, what are you…"

"Shh, honey. It's all right," Justin said. "Chet won't hurt you, but he's barely in control. He won't let his animal take over, but he's on edge after watching us make love with you and claim you. He wants to take you the way a wolf would take another wolf. Is that okay with you, Sam?"

"What do you mean?"

"On your hands and knees, mate," Chet commanded in a deep, gravelly voice and sighed when Sam complied. "Just relax, Sam."

Chet rubbed a hand over her luscious little backside then used both hands to hold her still. He covered her back with his large body and in that instant felt so damn big, strong, and masculine. She was so tiny he nearly hid her from view. Moving slightly, he pulled his hips back and thrust into her with one powerful surge. She cried out, and he cursed that he could have hurt her.

"Did I hurt you, darlin'? God, I'm sorry."

"No, you didn't hurt me. You feel so good inside me. More. Please, I need you. Fuck me! Hard!"

Chet growled and did what she asked. He set the pace hard and fast from the outset. After nuzzling her hair aside with his nose, he clamped his teeth against the back of her neck, showing his dominance. His muscles rippled as he set about sending her over into rapture before he followed her.

Wrapping an arm across her chest and holding her hip with the other, he shuttled his cock in and out of her pussy. The mewling and whimpering sounds she made only heightened his arousal, and the fact that she was unconsciously submitting to him filled him with joy. The loneliness and restlessness he had been feeling since the other members of the pack found their mates drifted away. When she pushed her ass back toward him and yelled as her cunt rippled around him with orgasmic pleasure, he thrust forward and bit down into her with his elongated teeth.

Her blood filled his mouth, and what he felt next blew him away. He could feel his brothers through their mating link as well as Sam. It felt like a strong rope ran from her heart out to all three of them. She was the center and anchor of them, and her bond with them only seemed to strengthen the bond he had with his brothers.

He howled against her neck and let orgasmic rapture take over. With his balls on fire he roared and shook as he climaxed, shooting his mate full of his cum.

Limbs shaking, he rolled to his side, taking Sam with him, and he buried his face in her hair, against her neck. He held her tightly against him as his heart filled with love for the one woman who would always be bonded to him.

"Are you okay, darlin'?" Chet asked, and when she didn't answer, he lifted his head and looked over her shoulder to see her face. "Sam?"

"She's asleep," Justin answered.

"Fuck. I love her so damn much. I'm never letting her go," Chet whispered to his brothers through their mental link.

"She's so fucking precious," Roan said with awe.

"Yes, she is. Did you feel the way she bound us together when Chet claimed her? That was…Wow! Just, fucking WOW!"

"I can't wait until we can make love with her together. I want in that sexy little ass so bad."

"We all want that, but the most important thing is to keep her safe. She is our responsibility now, but I still don't know anything about this Gerard Long guy or whoever it was watching her in the parking lot of the motel."

"We'll keep her safe," Chet reassured Justin. *"We can talk about it later. Right now we need to concentrate on our mate's needs. I'll go run a bath and clean her up so she's comfortable."* With that, Chet picked Sam up and carried her to the bathroom, his brothers following.

* * * *

Sam opened her eyes as warm water enveloped her. She blinked a few times to clear her blurry vision and looked up at Chet, who currently held her lovingly on his lap. Lowering her head, she breathed in his delicious, unique masculine scent and nuzzled into his chest with her nose.

"Hey, darlin', how are you feeling?"

"Good," she said with a contented sigh. "How did we get in here?"

"You passed out after making love with Chet, honey. He carried you in to the bath, thinking you would be more comfortable after cleaning up," Justin answered from beside her.

"Hmm, that's nice."

"Are you sore, sweetness?" Roan inquired.

"No, I'm fine. My muscles are a little stiff, but that's all."

"Are you hungry, honey?"

"Yeah, actually I am."

"Must be all that good loving we gave you, darlin'." Chet chuckled.

"I don't feel any different. Didn't you say I would see, hear, and smell better than before once we were mated?"

"Yeah, we did. I think you're just too tired to notice the difference. Let's go down to the kitchen and get you something to eat, and after a good night's sleep you'll feel much better," Justin suggested.

"Okay," Sam answered and reached for a bath sponge, which was quickly taken from her. "What…"

"We'll take care of you, sweetness. Just lie back and relax." Roan began to wash her.

"I'm perfectly capable of washing myself."

"We know you are, honey, but we like taking care of you." Justin helped Roan to wash her.

Tears pricked the back of her eyeballs. Closing her eyelids to hide her emotions, she let Justin and Roan wash her while Chet held her. Sam had never felt so loved and cared for in her life.

Peter would never have seen to it that she was comfortable. He would have climbed on top of her, not caring whether she found any pleasure in the act. Then he would have rolled over, totally ignoring her until he fell asleep.

These three men, part human and part animal, had given her more love and affection in the last four weeks than her husband had ever shown her in all the years of their marriage.

Chapter Ten

Roan led Sam into the dining room and sat down next to her at the long table. They were just in time for dinner, and the room was full of pack members. Smiling when Michelle, Keira, and Talia waved at Sam, he saw her blush and wave back. The men of the pack sniffed the air, and the cheers, howls, and well-wishes were yelled out to congratulate him and his brothers now that they were mated. The noise in the room diminished as Jonah rose from his seat at the head of the table.

"About damn time," Jonah growled good-naturedly. "I would like you all to welcome the newest member into our pack. We are pleased to have you with us, Samantha. You fit into this pack well and have become an invaluable member of this family."

"Thank you," Sam replied shyly and then sighed with relief.

Roan could tell she was glad when she was no longer the center of attention, because she relaxed into her chair when conversations started up again. When Angie and Cindy began to bring food to the table, Sam jumped up from her seat and hurried over to the kitchen counter. She helped the two women bring the food to the table and tried to whisper quietly to the elderly housekeeper, but he heard every word and knew the other *weres* of the pack could hear her as well.

"Angie, I would love to help you cook the food when I'm not working at the club. I love cooking and would like nothing better than to cook for people who would appreciate it."

"Thank you, Sam. That would be really nice. It's getting harder and harder to keep up with everything since the pack is expanding so rapidly, but I don't want you to overdo it since you're working as well. Why don't you discuss it with your mates and see what they have to say?" Angela suggested.

"I don't need to ask them to do anything, Angie. If I want to help you, then I will," she said with exasperation, and Roan saw her roll her eyes.

Roan felt the hackles on his neck rise as his mate unconsciously challenged him and his brothers. He was about to call her over and talk to her quietly, but Justin beat him to it.

"Samantha, come here."

She turned toward him and glared at Justin then turned her back on him. Hearing a couple of gasps from the younger Omegas, he looked at his pack members and glared at them to shut them up then turned back to Sam. He figured she could feel their eyes on her from the way she shifted uncomfortably from foot to foot, but she continued to ignore him, Justin, and Chet as she conversed with Angie.

"Sam, come here, now!" Justin demanded again, but this time he used his wolf, the power in his voice compelling her to follow his demand, so she would have trouble disobeying him.

Sam stomped over to Justin, placed her hands on her hips, and glared at him. "What?"

Roan had to hide his grin as her gaze slid from Justin to him and to Chet. Raising her chin with belligerence, she shifted her eyes back to Justin.

"You don't want to do this now, Justin. We are in a room filled with pack members and should do this in private," Roan suggested.

"Fuck, you're right," Justin replied. *"Okay, I guess we'll have to wait until we go back upstairs again."*

"Who says it was unconscious?" Sam answered. *"I knew exactly what I was doing. I know how dominant you three can be, but especially you and you."* Sam pointed a finger at Roan and Justin. *"If I want to help Angie and Cindy in the kitchen, then I will. You have no say in that. I will defer to you in the bedroom and when we are*

outside this house, but here I will have control of my own life. I can't let you take me over. You'll suffocate me just like he did. I won't have it. Is that clear?"

"Angie, please save us some dinner," Justin stated firmly, never taking his eyes off their mate. Rising to his feet, he growled and, with a lightning-fast move, slung Sam over his shoulder. He took the stairs three at a time. Roan and Chet hurried after them.

"Put me the fuck down," Sam yelled as she beat on Justin's back.

Roan couldn't help but laugh when Justin spanked her on the ass.

"Ow, that hurt."

"It was supposed to. I didn't know you had a potty mouth, honey, but I don't like it," Justin replied.

"Ooh, that is so hypocritical. You and your brothers swear all the time. How come you're allowed to and I'm not?"

"Because it sounds cheap and trashy coming from the mouth of such a beautiful woman."

"Well, it sounds just as bad coming out of your mouths. It's just my luck to find myself mated to men who have double standards," Sam grumbled. "Hey, why are we back in the bedroom? I'm hungry."

"You challenged us in front of the whole pack, sweetness. We can't let you get away with doing things like that," Roan said and sat down on the bed beside her after Justin lowered her into the middle.

"Look, I'm sorry. I know I shouldn't have said what I did, but I've had enough of being controlled by men. My ex eventually took me over until I was only a shell of my true self, and I can't—no, I won't go back there. I have only just found myself again, and I'm not going to let you take over my life like he did."

"Honey, we don't want to take over your life. As far as we are concerned your life is your own, but while that sicko is out there stalking you, we are going to do everything within our power to keep you safe. Yes, we like that you are submissive in the bedroom, and we love that you have the gumption to stand up for what you believe in, for what is right for you. But you have to remember we are part wolf,

Sam, and if you challenge us, whether consciously or not, we will rise to that challenge. It's what makes us who we are," Justin explained.

"Okay, I can understand that. I won't ever challenge you in front of the pack again, since you have no choice but to retaliate. So, what happens now?"

"Well, right now I want nothing more than to bury my hard cock into your pretty little pussy, but since I can hear your stomach growling, I guess we'll have to put that off for a little while," Justin replied. "But as soon as dinner is over, we will be coming back up here and making love with you."

Sam gulped and drew in a ragged breath, which they all heard. She gave a slight nod of her head. Chet took her hand in his, helped her from the bed, and led the way back down to the dining room. Roan noticed she kept her head bent and her cheeks were tinged a pink hue when they entered the room. She didn't speak until their meal was over, and that was only to offer to help Angie clean up the kitchen, along with Michelle, Keira, and Talia.

Just as the women finished up in the kitchen, one of the young Omegas burst into the room.

"There's been a perimeter break! The garden shed in the northeast corner is on fire."

The male pack members as well as Keira rushed out of the house and took off toward the back of the property. Greg, Jake, and Devon took the lead, and Roan and his brothers surrounded their Alphas in case it was a trap to lure them out into the open. Chris, Blayk, and James were instructed to stay at the house to keep an eye on the women and Michelle's baby.

He sniffed the air and tried to get the scent of the intruder, but the smell of smoke and gas permeated the air, drowning everything else out. His wolf made his presence known and tried to get him to shift, but he pushed his animal back down. Until he knew what they were up against he intended to stay in control. The last thing he wanted was for a human to find out about their species.

The Omegas had already started fighting the fire with garden hoses, as well as buckets of water, but the flames were too intense. Roan dug his cell phone out of his pocket and called 9-1-1. By the time he hung up, a truck was on its way, but the fire was threatening the surrounding trees. Roan looked back toward the house. The fire had a long way to go, but the wind would eventually push it toward the house. He took a bucket of water from one of the Omegas and threw it toward the shed. Something crashed down inside and threw sparks into his face. Roan winced and stepped backward, coughing as smoke caught in his lungs.

Jonas called out through the common pack link for Chris, Blayk, and James. *"Come quickly. We need to keep it from spreading."*

The others came running moments later. Roan was glad for their help, but he felt uneasy. As the fire truck came screaming down the road, he stepped back from the flames and scanned the area using his enhanced wolf sight. Nothing. He didn't see one fucking thing out of place.

"I don't like this," Roan muttered as the hair on his nape stood on end and his gut dropped with dread.

"Neither do I," Justin replied.

"Why would someone set the garden shed on fire?" Chet asked with bewilderment.

"Shit! This was done as a distraction. Get the hell back to the house and make sure our women are safe!" Jonah yelled.

* * * *

Sam had just settled on the sofa in the living room with Michelle and Talia after Chris, Blayk, and James raced out to help the others with the fire. Dread settled in the pit of her stomach, but she didn't let it show. The other women didn't seem worried. Michelle yawned and finished feeding baby Stefan and then placed him over her shoulder to burp. The woman looked exhausted, and Sam knew that she couldn't have had much sleep the previous night. Her head slumped onto the back of the sofa and her eyes closed.

"Why don't you give me Stefan and go and have a bath or shower? Let me take him for a while so you can relax," Sam suggested.

Michelle opened her eyes and looked at her hopefully. "Are you sure? He's been very finicky the last few days. I think he's cutting teeth."

"Yes, I'm sure. Take Talia with you. She looks like she could use an early night."

"Gee, thanks so much," Talia replied with a snicker. "These damn hormones are driving me crazy."

"Wait until you have a baby to care for and then you'll know what tired is," Michelle said around another yawn.

"Go, and don't worry if you don't have the energy to come back down. Stefan's safe with me."

"I know he is, Sam. Thank you. Just hand him over to one of my mates when they get back."

Sam didn't watch the women leave the room. She only had eyes for the precious bundle in her arms. Rubbing his small back, she was surprised when he let out a belch loud enough to rival a full-grown male, and she laughed.

"I'll bet that feels a lot better." Placing a kiss on his head, she inhaled the sweet scent of baby and talcum powder. What she wouldn't give to hold her own child like this. If she was blessed, maybe one day soon she would conceive again.

She caught movement from the corner of her eye and turned her head. She froze and gasped for air as she felt the blood in her head drain away. Willing the lightheadedness away, she took a deep breath and then another as she stared in horror at the man who had been her nemesis for nearly six months.

Gerard Long stood in the doorway of the living room, smiling at her evilly with a long-bladed knife in his hand. He moved toward her, and she quickly gained her feet, backing away and searching for someone to help her. Of course, everyone was either upstairs or outside battling a fire. She could hear Cindy and Angie in the kitchen but didn't want to call out and put them in danger.

"I've waited a long time for this moment, bitch. You and I are going to have so much fun."

Sam's heart pounded fearfully in her chest, but she didn't let that fear control her. She needed to keep a clear head so she could protect Stefan. She would give her own life before she would let Gerard harm the baby. Slowly working her way around the sectional sofa, she kept her eyes on him. He followed her every move but didn't stop coming toward her. When she had worked her way around to the back of the couch and he stood away from the exit, she took the only chance she had.

Wrapping her arms around Stefan and hunching over him to protect his small body, she spun and took off. She ran as she had never run before, but she could hear Gerard close behind her. She reached the door to the carport, but as she flung it open, searing pain stabbed through her back. Stumbling in agony, she pushed the discomfort away and concentrated on getting Stefan to safety.

Glancing back over her shoulder, she saw Gerard laughing insanely as he leaned against the doorjamb. Then he moved back inside and out of sight. Her knees gave out, and she sobbed with anger because she couldn't push her body to keep going.

Roan seemed to materialize out of nowhere. "Roan," she screamed, "take the baby and keep him safe."

Roan enveloped her and Stefan in his arms. Sighing with relief that Michelle's baby was safe, she let the darkness take her

* * * *

Roan took the lead back toward the den. Just as he reached the beginning of the landscaped gardens, Sam burst out through the door with Michelle's baby in her arms. She was covered in blood. He roared with fear and fury and leaped the last few yards toward her.

He reached her just in time to catch her as she stumbled toward the ground. Scooping her and the baby into his arms, he cradled her in close to his chest.

"Sam, you're covered in blood. Where are you hurt?" he yelled with terror.

When she didn't answer him he gently kneeled on the ground, careful not to jostle her and hurt her further. He handed the baby to Brock as he came up beside him and began to look for Sam's injury. Turning her on her side in case she got sick, he examined his woman, panic stricken when he found blood seeping from what looked like a knife wound on her back.

"The other women are safe and unharmed. They didn't see what happened, but the scent of human male is prevalent throughout the house. Pack members are searching for the fucker," Mikhail said in a deep, harsh voice as he hurried toward them. "Sam was watching the baby so Michelle could take a shower. The other women were in the kitchen, and as you already know, Keira was out with us."

"Fuck! We left the women unprotected and fell for the oldest trick in the book," Jonah said angrily.

"Blayk, get your bag. Samantha has been stabbed," Mikhail called through the common pack link.

Roan was only vaguely aware of what was going on around him. He was too busy trying to stem the blood flow from the knife injury in Sam's back. He growled when anyone other than his brothers got too close to his mate. He and his wolf were furious that his woman had been hurt.

"Roan, you have to let Blayk take a look at our mate," Justin stated calmly. *"We need him to attend her so she doesn't lose too much blood. Pick her up and bring her to the infirmary."*

Roan could see Justin's relief when he gently picked Sam up off the ground, being careful not to jostle her and hurt her any more than she already was. He walked quickly to the doctor's office which had been set up only in the last twelve months and thanked God his Alphas had had the foresight to do so. The last thing he wanted was to have to call for an ambulance or to rush Sam to the hospital. He didn't want her off the property or out of his sight or strangers attending to his mate.

Carefully placing Sam on the bed on her side, he stepped back as Blayk moved toward her. The sight of his cousin and the pack doctor cutting away his woman's shirt was one of the hardest things he had to watch. Justin and Chet came to stand beside him, and he knew neither of them would be leaving this room anytime soon, just like he wasn't.

Blayk prepared a syringe full of painkillers and shot it into Sam's arm. She groaned and was about to turn over onto her stomach, but Roan stepped forward, took ahold of her shoulder, and knelt at her side.

"Shh, sweetness, you're going to be all right. Don't move, and let Blayk fix you up."

"Shit, where's the baby?" Sam asked, panicked.

"He's back with his mother, honey," Justin replied. "Now be a good girl and stay still for Blayk."

"Samantha, I've given you a shot of pain meds, but I have to give you another so I can disinfect the wound and stitch you up. I'm sorry, honey, but it's going to hurt," Blayk explained.

"S'okay," Sam slurred.

Roan was thankful that her pain medication was kicking in. He could tell by her glazed-over eyes, dilated pupils, and slurred speech that she wasn't used to taking medication or just had a low tolerance for the stuff. He held her shoulder in a firm grip and placed his other hand at her waist. Justin placed a hand on her hip and Chet placed a hand on her thigh to hold her still. He nodded at Blayk to let his cousin know they would keep her steady.

Sam squeaked when Blayk began to inject the local anesthetic and tried to lift her arm, but Roan stopped her by clasping her hand. She dug her nails into the back of his hand and punctured his skin, but he didn't flinch. Even though he wasn't responsible for her wound, he felt as if they had failed their mate. If they hadn't pulled everyone to the site of the fire they could have fought the human and kept Sam safe. He wondered if Long had been the one to wreck their security system so he could gain entry to their land. If they had been on hand, Sam would probably now be tucked up in bed with them or on the sofa in the living room talking to the other women.

"Fucking hell! I hate this," Justin spat through their link.

"We should have known it wasn't a coincidence that this happened when the security system was down," Chet added angrily.

"S'not your fault," Sam muttered as Blayk began to stitch her skin back together. "You couldn't have known the fire was set to distract you all."

"We should have known it was a setup, sweetness. We never leave the women unattended, and we should have been even more vigilant with the alarm system down," Roan said vehemently.

Blayk finally finished suturing Sam's flesh, and as he tied off the thread, her hand went lax in Roan's. He glanced down and sighed with relief. Their little mate was fast asleep. She hadn't been able to fight the effects of the pain medication any longer.

"Keep this waterproof bandage on, but keep an eye out for blood seepage," Blayk said. "That could mean she's pulled her stitches. Call me if your mate experiences too much pain and I'll give her another shot. No strenuous activities or heavy lifting, and make sure she gets plenty of rest. You can take her up to your rooms."

"Have they found who attacked her yet?" Roan asked.

"No," Jonah growled. "Don't worry, we'll get this bastard. He can't have gone far, and when we find him, he's a dead man. Just concentrate on looking after your mate."

Roan turned back to Blayk. "How long before the threads come out?"

"It depends on how fast Samantha heals. Now that you've all claimed her it should be around three days."

"Thanks, Blayk." Justin watched as Roan gently lifted Sam into his arms. Chet moved in and covered her with a blanket, and Roan left the clinic.

"Justin, did you find out what happened from your mate?" Jonah asked as they stepped inside.

"No, we'll have to wait until she wakes. Sorry, Alpha, but I don't think our mate deals well with pain medication," Justin replied.

"I want a full account as soon as she's conscious. Call me and we'll come to her. The last thing she is going to want to do is move around too much, and I don't want to cause her any unnecessary discomfort," Jonah said.

"Thanks, Jonah, I'll call as soon as she wakes."

Roan continued carrying Sam up the stairs to their room on the third floor. Chet had gone on ahead to get the bed ready for their mate.

Striding toward the bed, he gently lowered her and cursed when she moaned. Being careful of her wound, he and his brothers removed her clothes and tucked her into bed. He undressed, climbed in beside her, and pulled her until she was lying half on top of him, her cheek resting on his chest, her breasts against his belly and her legs entangled with his. Roan didn't want her inadvertently rolling onto her back and hurting herself. He had every intention of keeping her in his arms all night long.

Justin and Chet stripped off and climbed into bed, too. She was surrounded by them, and he vowed no one would ever get to her and hurt her again.

Chapter Eleven

Sam woke with her back driving her crazy. If she could have reached it, she would have torn at her itchy skin to relieve the irritation. Sitting up suddenly, she looked about the room. Sighing with relief she realized she was back in her room in the pack house. Then the events of the previous night came rushing back.

She gingerly arose from the bed and carefully pulled on some clothes and left the suite. She was down the stairs and in the dining room before she knew where she had been heading. All the people looked up at her with concern as she scanned the room frantically. Her knees began to buckle when she spied baby Stefan sitting on Michelle's lap.

"Thank God," she whispered and reached out to steady her weak body.

Justin was at her side a moment later and lifted her up into his arms. "What's wrong, honey? Are you in pain?"

"No. I just had to make sure Stefan was safe," she replied and hid her face against his chest.

"Bring your mate over to the table, Justin. I'd like to have a word with her," Jonah commanded.

Justin carried her over to the seat Mikhail vacated and sat down with Sam on his lap. He held her gently but securely, and she was appreciative because she was shaking like a leaf.

"Here, have some coffee, honey. That will help warm you up again." Angie shoved a mug of coffee into her hands.

Sam clutched it gratefully and let the warmth penetrate her cold palms and fingers. "Thanks, Angie."

"Sam, I want you to tell me what happened last night," Jonah commanded in a gentle voice.

"I–I was sitting in the living room on the sofa, holding Stefan until he fell asleep, so Michelle could take a shower. I heard about the fire, but I knew you would all have it under control, and I so love cuddling with Stefan, so I just stayed where I was. Talia had also taken the chance to bathe, and Keira was outside with you all," she explained then took a deep, steadying breath. "He came after me. I'm so sorry. I should never have come here. I've put you all in danger. I'll leave as soon as I can pack my stuff."

"You aren't going anywhere, *mate!*" Justin commanded in a gentle voice. "Who was it, Samantha?"

"Gerard Long. He came inside when everyone was gone, and he was holding a knife in his hand. I had to try and get away. I couldn't let him hurt Stefan. Oh, God," she sobbed. "I'm so sorry."

Hiding her face against Justin's chest, she gave in to her sobs of fear, anxiety, and guilt. The last thing she had wanted to do was put any of these people in jeopardy. She had been so selfish, mating these three men when she wasn't safe. Now she had put them all in danger, too. She couldn't live with that. If Gerard had hurt Stefan, she would never be able to live with her conscience.

"Samantha, you have nothing to be sorry for," Jonah said quietly. "If anyone is to blame for what happened, it is us and the bastard who attacked you. It was our duty to protect you. I knew he could come after you, and then I fell for the oldest trick in the book. A diversion. Please, don't leave. Stay here with your mates. We promise you will be safe here. The new security system will be installed today, and there is no way in hell anyone else will ever be able to get in here without one of us knowing about it. The only reason we didn't smell that bastard was because of all the smoke from the fire. I want to thank you for protecting my child. If you hadn't been there, I don't know what would have happened. Stefan could be dead right now."

"You shouldn't be thanking me. It's my fault that Gerard was here," she sobbed. Then she turned to her mates. "I can't believe you told them. How could you?"

Trying to push off Justin's lap, she gave up when he wouldn't release her. She let her forehead bump onto his chest.

"We only told the others what they needed to know to help keep you safe. And it's not your fault, honey. You didn't ask him to follow you or come after you, so get that thought out of your head, right now. You can't control what other people think or do, now can you?" Justin asked.

"No."

"That's right. So don't you dare go running to try and protect all of us. It's you we should be protecting. I'm sorry we failed in our job to keep you safe, but there is no fucking way it will ever happen again," Justin affirmed.

"Okay," she sighed and then sniffed.

"Thanks for keeping my baby safe, Sam." Michelle sobbed emotively.

"Sure." Sam brushed aside the praise, still not comfortable since she was to blame.

"Why don't you have some breakfast, darlin'? Then you can go and take a shower," Chet suggested.

"Hmm, sounds good, cause I'm starting to get hungry." Sam's stomach took that opportune moment to growl loudly. Everyone around the table burst into laughter, which helped to lighten the mood, but she knew she wouldn't be comfortable until the threat of Gerard Long was no more.

After breakfast Justin helped her to stand. Roan and Chet rose to their feet as well.

"Make sure you don't get those stitches wet, Samantha," Blayk reminded her with a smile. She waved at him and smiled back to let him know she would abide his dictates. She let her men lead her out of the room.

Justin pulled her into the bathroom after him, turned the shower on, and began to undress her. Sam slapped at his hand.

"I can undress myself. Please, just leave me be. I need some time alone."

"We aren't going to let you hide from us, Samantha. I know you still feel guilty about what happened, but you shouldn't. You had nothing to do with this."

"How the fuck can you say that? If I hadn't come here, baby Stefan would never have been put into any danger," she said angrily, her breath panting from between her lips.

"I don't want to hear you speak like that again, Sam. If you do, I will put you over my knee and spank your ass." Justin glared at her through narrowed eyes.

"You just fucking try it, bu…Put me down! What the hell do you think you're doing?" she screeched from her upside-down position over his shoulder. His hands held her firmly so she couldn't wiggle around and pull her stitches.

"I warned you, honey, and you decided to see how far you can push me. Well, I'm up for the challenge. Are you, Sam?"

Sam beat against his back, but she might as well have been banging on a brick wall. Her world spun, and the next thing she knew, she was on the bed flat on her stomach. But the whole time he maneuvered her not once did she feel any pain from her wound site.

"Don't fight me, Sam, I don't want you to pull your stitches," Justin demanded in a firm voice.

"Ugh! I've had it with you! Let me go."

She would never have admitted it in a million years, but she liked fighting back against him. She liked the feel of his big hands pinning her down. From the glitter in Justin's eyes, she thought he enjoyed it just as much.

"Hold her down and make sure she doesn't hurt herself," Justin commanded his brothers.

Now three sets of hands pinned her to the mattress, and nothing she did made them let her go. She tried to buck and twist but could hardly move as their gentle hands held her firmly. Excited arousal shot through her stomach as she dug her nails into Roan's hand.

"Stop fighting, you little hellcat." Justin pulled her sweats and panties down her legs.

Her pussy pulsed at the sudden exposure. She got as far as saying, "I'll show you a hell—oh God."

The first smack to her ass froze her squirming body with shock. It hadn't been hard enough to cause her pain, but it was forceful enough to heat her skin. The heat travelled around from her ass cheek into her pussy, making her sheath clench and release a gush of cream.

"Mmm, I think our little darlin' likes getting her ass smacked. I can smell your cream from here, Sam," Chet stated in a low, rumbling voice.

Sam gasped when another smack landed on her bottom. She bit her lip to hold back the moan bubbling up in her chest. *How the hell can I get turned on by a spanking?* Every time Justin's hand landed on her butt, he then soothed his palm over the heat. She was so turned on that she was only vaguely aware that she was arching her hips up into his touch.

"Turn her over," Justin commanded.

Sam found herself turned over, propped up on pillows so the wound on her back was protected. Her gaze met Justin's heated stare, and she felt singed right down to her toes.

"Do you have any idea how fucking sexy you are?" he rasped.

"See there. That's what I mean. You are such a f…hypocrite. How come you're allowed to swear and if I do I get a spanking?"

"Because we aren't as good with words as you are, honey. We also know that you like to be dominated and a spanking turns you on. You are so full of fire and passion, Sam. Do you think we don't see that? We see your fire every time you look at us. And don't tell me you didn't goad us on purpose. You love what we do to you, don't you, honey?"

"How the hell would you know what I like and don't like? You've only ever taken me once," she said breathily.

"That sounds like another challenge to me, Justin. What do you think?" Roan inquired, giving her a lascivious smile and wink.

"I think you're right. You have no idea what you've just done, honey. I hope you're up to facing the consequences." He then leaned down over her, wrapped his arms around her legs, and opened them wide.

"Oh God," she managed to get out just before Justin's mouth met her pussy.

Sam cried out as Justin's tongue swept through her wet slit, and she bowed up off the bed.

"Hold her still, damn it. I don't want her pulling those stitches." She sobbed as his breath and the vibrations of his voice contacting with her pussy made her shiver.

"I want your cock. Give it to me *now*," she demanded in a husky voice.

"Bring her down to me," Justin commanded.

Sam whimpered as she was moved down the bed until her head was just below the middle and her feet were resting against the foot of the bed frame. Lifting her head with curiosity, she felt Chet and Roan move off the bed and glanced over to see they were each removing their clothes. Her gaze connected with Justin's, and she let her eyes wander over his naked body, wondering when he had removed his own garments. Getting on the bed beside her with his head near her feet, he pulled her over onto her side until her face was level with his crotch, all the while protecting her back.

"I need to feel your mouth on me, honey," he rasped. He held the base of his hard dick and brushed the head over her lips.

Inhaling his musky scent and spying the drop of fluid on the tip, she leant forward and licked over his slit. He rewarded her by groaning loudly, and then he lowered his head back to her pussy. Mewling with delight at this new position and the pleasure of having his tongue sliding through her folds, she opened her mouth and sucked him in.

"Oh, fuck yeah! That's it, Sam. Shit! Your mouth feels like heaven, honey. Suck me down," Justin moaned.

With his flavor exploding on her tongue, she hollowed her cheeks and began to greedily suckle on the tip of his cock. Moaning around his hard flesh, she began to move her mouth up and down his length as he laved her clit. Justin made sexy growling sounds as he lapped up her cream, and she bobbed her head over his cock faster, determined to make him climax before she did.

Only vaguely aware of the mattress dipping behind her, she concentrated on giving him as much pleasure as he was giving her but froze when another set of hands began to massage the cheeks of her ass. Releasing Justin's cock with a pop, she turned her head and looked over her shoulder to find Roan there.

"What are you doing?" she asked breathlessly.

"I'm getting you ready, sweetness," he replied in a deep, gravelly voice.

"Ready for what?"

"We are all going to take you at the same time, Sam. Now, turn back around and suck Justin's cock," he directed and gave her ass a playful tap.

"I don't…"

"Do you trust us, honey?" Justin asked.

"Yes."

"Then just relax and let us take care of you. We won't hurt you, darlin'," Chet said from above her, and she tilted her head back to see him staring at her as he lay across the top of the bed.

She groaned loudly when Justin lowered his head back to her pussy, licking over her clit, and she took his cock back into her mouth. Arching her hips toward him when he slid a digit into her vagina and lightly sucked on her sensitive bundle of nerves, she laved the underside of his cock with her tongue. Hearing him moan with pleasure only made her more determined to send him into climax, but she stilled again as Roan pushed the tip of a finger into her ass.

She whimpered around Justin's cock as nerves she hadn't known existed zinged pulses of electrical sparks through her body.

"Don't tense up, sweetness. Let me in. Take a deep breath, Sam," Roan crooned to her. "That's it. God, you're so fucking sexy. Try to push my finger out. Oh yeah. See? Your body craves having something in your ass now."

Beside herself with hunger, Sam couldn't believe the pleasurable sensations running through her. Roan's finger was now all the way inside her ass, and with Justin's in her pussy, she felt so full and needy.

"Two fingers now, sweet. Yes, that's it, try and push me out. Fuck! Her ass is so tight, I can't wait to feel what it's going to do to my cock," Roan rasped.

"Stop, honey," Justin growled and pulled his hips away from her, her mouth making a popping sound as she released him.

"Why did you stop?"

"Because I was too close to coming, and I want to be buried in your hot, tight pussy when I do."

"I have three fingers in her now. She's ready."

Sam was about to sit up, but three sets of hands stopped her.

"Just relax, darlin'. We'll do all the work and take care of you," Chet said through clenched teeth.

She looked up at him, and the hunger in his eyes made her burn even more. Sam was so horny, her body was one big aching mass of nerves and her pussy was leaking copious amounts of her juices.

Justin maneuvered until he was sitting on the side of the bed. He lifted her up using his powerful muscles and brought her onto his lap, until she was straddling his thighs, facing him.

"We'll take this nice and slow, honey. Tell us if it's too much for you to handle. Okay?"

Sam gave a nod and then closed her eyes as he slowly lowered her onto his hard cock. She moaned with delight as her cunt enveloped his erection. Justin took his time with her. He didn't surge into her with one pump, but instead he thrust his hips slowly, slipping his cock in and out of her, gaining depth with every move. When he was embedded in her vagina, his dick touching her cervix, he pulled her tight against his chest. The feel of her nipples brushing against his chest hair made her groan.

Another pair of hands smoothed over her shoulders and down to her back, being careful not to touch her injury, until they reached her ass. Kneading the globes of her butt, Roan kissed her on the shoulder and bent until his head was next to hers, his chin resting on her shoulder.

"I'll take things easy with you, sweetness, but don't hesitate to tell me to stop if you need to. All right?" Roan whispered against her ear.

Sam shivered as his warm, moist breath caressed her sensitive skin, and since she didn't think she could answer just now, she nodded instead.

"Take a deep breath, Sam, and hold it. When you exhale, push back against me, sweetheart." His voice had a deep cadence.

Closing her eyes tight, she did what he said and pushed back. The head of his cock began to push against her anus, and then he popped through her tight sphincter muscle.

"Breathe in again, sweetness, and push back once more," Roan told her.

"Open your eyes, honey," Justin demanded.

She looked up at Justin, her internal muscles clenching in reaction to the heat she saw in his gaze as he looked at her.

"You are so gorgeous, Sam. Just relax and let us pleasure you." Justin gasped, holding her hips firmly.

"Fuck! Your ass is so tight, sweetheart, but by God you feel so fucking good," Roan rasped.

"It burns," Sam moaned.

"Do you want me to stop?"

"No! I need you, all of you, to love me. Shit, you make me feel so good."

"We've only just started, darlin'," Chet's voice rumbled from beside her.

Looking up and to the side, she found that Chet was kneeling on the bed beside her, stroking his cock in the palm of his hand. Licking her lips, she imagined what he tasted like, and the thought ramped up her desire even more.

"Do you want my cock in that sweet mouth, darlin'?"

"Yes, move closer," she urged him.

"I'm all the way in, sweetness. How are you feeling?" Roan moaned.

"Like I'm stuffed full of cock." She giggled breathlessly.

"You're such a sassy little thing. Open your mouth for me, Sam," Chet demanded and brushed the tip of his hard cock against her lips.

Not needing to be told twice, she opened her mouth and licked all around the crown of his cock. Loving the taste and wanting more, she sucked him in as far as she could handle and began to bob up and down his length, paying particular attention to the sensitive spot she had found on Justin's cock when she had gone down on him.

"Oh yeah, darlin', that feels so good," Chet groaned.

She moaned around Chet's dick when Justin lifted her slightly from his lap and thrust his rod up into her cunt. As he withdrew again, Roan slid from her ass then surged back in. With every pump of their hips she bobbed her head, keeping in time with them while sucking on Chet's penis.

Every time they advanced and retreated, sending shards of pleasure coursing through her body, they increased the pace. She kept up with them and hollowed out her cheeks with every pass over

Chet's cock and slurped back down over his flesh, trying to take him to the back of her throat.

"You don't need to do that, darlin'," Chet moaned. "Don't go too far. What you're doing so far feels like heaven."

She mewled around his dick as Justin and Roan ramped up the speed of their cocks, shuttling in and out of her ass and pussy. Never had she felt such exquisite friction or such a deep connection to three people in her life. Her heart filled with joy as they made love with her tenderly and gave her hope for the future. Tears of emotion pricked her eyeballs, and her breath hitched in her chest when she inhaled through her nose. A lump of happiness formed in her heart, and she gasped around Chet's penis. The emptiness she had carried around for so long slowly dissipated until she was so full her emotions began to bubble over. Warmth permeated her pussy and womb, travelling up to her chest and filling her soul.

Justin shifted a hand from her hips, tweaked a nipple between his finger and thumb, then caressed all the way down to her slit. He tapped lightly on her clit, sending waves of molten lava through her extremities, and then he gently squeezed her little nubbin and sent her over the edge into bliss.

Sam screamed, the sound muffled by Chet's cock still in her mouth, shaking and jerking uncontrollably as she climaxed.

"Get ready, Sam. I'm gonna come," Chet rumbled.

His cock swelled and jerked in her mouth, and she swallowed rapidly as his cum spewed from the tip of his penis, onto her tongue, and down her throat. Just as he pulled away, Roan and Justin began pounding in and out of her holes, their skin making slapping sounds as their bodies connected with hers. Justin squeezed a little more firmly on her clit. Throwing her head back, she screamed long and loud as another wave of nirvana swept over her, sending her into another climax. Roan yelled as he thrust his cock into her ass, his motion freezing as he held her hip firmly in one hand. Feeling his penis pulsing deep inside her only enhanced her own pleasure. Justin followed a moment later, shouting out as he spilled his seed into her cunt.

Spasms continued to rock her body, her pussy and ass quaking until finally the last wave died. Slumping against Justin, she closed her eyes and sighed with satiation.

"I love you, honey." Sam heard Justin's declaration, and then his two brothers repeated his words, but she was already sinking into the land of Nod and could only smile in return.

Chapter Twelve

Finished with collecting dirty glass and other dishes, Sam headed back to the kitchen. The whole back end of the Aztec Club was spotlessly clean, and the kitchen was a chef's dream. She had just found out that the club had been rebuilt only recently. Keira's brother had tried to kill her to get ahold of her money and had set the club on fire and then kidnapped her.

Trouble seemed to follow the women who were fated to be mates of the men of the Friess Pack. She'd heard Michelle's and Talia's stories as well, and even though it made her feel a little better to know she wasn't the only one to bring trouble to town, she still wasn't comfortable knowing she was putting others in danger.

Roan gave her a smile and wink as he passed by, and a few moments later, Chet following after his brother, caught her eye, and grinned at her. Sam loaded the dishwasher, washed her hands, and went back to cook the next order up. At the moment the menu offered only the usual fare such as burgers and fries, but she had plans to offer much healthier and more appetizing food. She would have to run it by her mates and probably the Alphas as well, but she had big plans for this place now that her men had relented and let her return.

It had been nearly four weeks since Gerard had attacked her in the pack house. It had taken a lot of persuasion on her part to get back in this kitchen. Now that she was comfortable with the men in her life being werewolves, the rest of the pack had relaxed, too, and she didn't jump or startle when a wolf came across her path any longer. She had actually gone to watch her mates and pack members shift on the night of a full moon, and even though she had been embarrassed at first, forgetting everyone would have to remove their clothes, the sight of a nude body now no longer made her cheeks turn pink.

Ringing the bell to let the other waitstaff know the order was up, she looked for the next one, but the hooks were empty. Glancing at her watch, she realized it was now after ten p.m. and no more food orders would be taken, so she set about cleaning up.

It took Sam just under an hour to clean the kitchen until it was sparkling, and since she had been working from midday, her feet were aching. She grabbed a bottle of water and made her way toward the back door. She just needed a quiet moment to breathe in some fresh country air. Slipping through the rear door, she sat down on the step and sipped at her beverage.

Hearing a shuffle of feet against the concrete in the alley, she looked intently into the darkness. Her eyesight was a lot better since she had been claimed by her mates, and even though she couldn't see who it was, she could make out the silhouette of a tall male walking toward her. Sam stood and reached out behind her, feeling for the door handle as she stepped back into the door. Just as her hand met the cool metal of the knob, the male leapt toward her and pulled her against him. Squeaking with fright, she looked up into the demonic, evil eyes of Gerard Long. She opened her mouth to scream. No more than a squeak emerged before it was muffled by his large hand covering her mouth and nose.

Dropping the bottle, she twisted and pushed against him, using all the strength she could muster, but he was much larger and stronger than she was, so her efforts were futile. Spreading her legs to regain her balance, she lifted her knee, aiming for his crotch, but he moved quickly and she only connected with his thigh.

"Nice try, you little bitch. You'll pay for that," he said coldly.

Sam fought against him, but nothing she did seemed to make a difference. She was beginning to feel lightheaded and brought her hands up to claw at the hand covering her mouth and nose. Just as stars began to form before her eyes, she used her mind and called to her mates.

"Roan, Chet, Justin, help me," she screamed into their mind link as a prick stabbed into her neck, just before her body slumped and she passed out.

* * * *

"Sam, where are you?" Justin asked frantically. *"Sam?"*

"Fuck! What the hell is going on? Where is she?" Roan said through their link.

Justin and his brothers hurried out from behind the bar, heedless of the fact they had customers to serve.

"She's not in the kitchen?" Chet asked as he passed.

"She's not in the office either," Roan said. *"Where the hell could she be?"*

"For fuck's sake. Both of you calm down and use your wolf senses. She's outside." Justin urgently followed their mate's scent.

"What the hell is she doing outside? We told her not to go anywhere without letting us know first. I am going to paddle her ass when we find her," Chet said vehemently.

"We have to find her first." Justin desperately sniffed the air near the back door to the club. *"I can smell human male mixed with her, and the scent is familiar. It's the same smell she had on her after she was stabbed."*

"It has to be that motherfucker, Long."

"I'm going to change and see if my wolf can get a fix on Sam." Justin quickly began to remove his clothes. *"Keep a watch out, and if anyone comes near, make sure they don't see me."*

"Sam, can you hear me, darlin'?" Chet called to their mate through their mental link. *"Fucking hell. Nothing. What has that bastard done to her?"*

"Take it easy, Chet. You have to get ahold of yourself. We need to keep cool heads if we are going to find our mate and have her back in our arms," Roan said quietly.

"I have her scent, and I can smell a chemical of some sort. I think he's drugged her. I'm going to see which way they went." Justin leapt away and disappeared out of the alley. He followed the trail to where a car had been parked. Sniffing the ground, he chuffed with frustration, knowing he wouldn't be able to track any further. He looked around, making sure no one saw him in his wolf form, and headed back to his brothers.

"Should we call for backup?" Chet snarled. *"Did you find anything?"*

"No. He had a car waiting," Justin explained. *"Her scent's gone, and yes, call Greg, Jake, and Devon. We need someone to take over the bar. Not that I care, our mate is more important than the club."*

"I don't give a fuck about the bar. We could just kick everyone out and close up."

"Yes, I'll get everyone out. Shit. I'd better get back in there before someone starts a riot," Chet snapped, heading back inside.

"I'll call in Greg, Jake, and Devon. They can help us track our mate. It won't be long before they get here." Roan sighed with frustration.

"Wait! Get Greg to run a check on Long. We need to know what his license plate number is." Justin's bones began to pop, his muscles contorting as he changed back to his human form. *"See if he can get Jarrod to find him through the police database. Since he's the sheriff and a* were *as well as a pack member, he won't hesitate to help out. Just get Jake and Devon here, ASAP,"* Justin snarled, pulling his clothes back on as Roan handed them to him one piece at a time.

"Jarrod, I need your help," Roan called to Jarrod through the common pack mind link. *"I want you to run a Gerard Long through the system. He has our mate. If you can find his registration details, I want you to put an APB out on him."*

"Sure, I'll get back to you as soon as I have something," Jarrod replied.

"Jake and Devon are here," Chet informed his brothers from inside the bar. *"We can head to the sheriff's office and be on hand as soon as Jarrod has any information."*

"Okay, let's meet at the truck. I want the vehicle close so we can head out as soon as Jarrod gets a reading on the fucker." Justin headed out front.

Chet was already in the driver's seat with the engine running when Justin and Roan converged on the vehicle. He took off before they had their doors closed. Moments later the truck screeched to a halt outside the sheriff's office. All three of them were out of the truck and inside seconds later.

"Have you got anything?" Justin called out as soon as he stepped inside.

"Yeah," his cousin Jarrod answered. "He's driving a silver late-model sedan. I've already put out an APB on him. If he's anywhere close, one of my deputies will spot him and call in."

"Fuck! I can't stand the thought of Sam being with that bastard. She has to be so scared. I'll rip his fucking head off his shoulders when I find him," Justin snarled.

"Hang on a minute," Jarrod said and turned to the radio. "Go ahead, Malcolm, what have you got?"

"I just spotted the car you put an alert on. It's heading south on 550 toward Nageezi. There was a woman in the passenger seat. I'm following from a distance, awaiting further instructions," Malcolm stated.

"Just keep them in sight. Do not apprehend, repeat, do not apprehend. I'll let you know what's happening soon," Jarrod said and signed off. Turning toward Justin and his brothers, he pinned them with a look.

"You know we can't let him get away with taking our mate, Jarrod. If it was your mate, you'd want to get to her and keep her safe.

We'll let you and your brothers be backup, but we are the ones going in to rescue her," Justin said vehemently.

"We don't even know for sure where this guy is taking your woman. He may decide to drive through the night," Jarrod suggested.

"No, I don't think he will. He's been after Sam for six months already. I think he'll stop the first opportunity he can. He's probably got someplace all set up in preparation," Roan said.

"Why the hell didn't you tell me about this shit before? I could have had this Long guy watched before now," Jarrod snapped.

"First of all, Sam didn't want anyone to know what was going on. She had a conniption when she found out that we told Jonah, Mikhail, and Brock that she was on the run." Justin took a breath when his wolf made itself known in his garbled voice. "Secondly, you know as well as everyone else in the pack that we have been working our way up to the rank of Beta. We are going to handle this alone so that our Alphas know we can handle more responsibility."

"Jonah already knows you and your brothers are Betas," Jarrod said. "He was going to announce it on the next full moon. You don't have to prove anything to anyone. I understand your need to rescue your mate, but don't go in half-cocked and put her in even more jeopardy. We are trained to handle this sort of thing. I want you to promise to call out if you need any help. You can't risk the life of your mate with your stubborn ass."

"You think I don't know that? I'm not stupid, Jarrod. I'll call you and Malcolm if we need help, but right now I need to go after my mate," Justin snapped and slammed out the door, heading toward the truck. His angry strides ate up the distance rapidly. He jumped into the truck and barely waited for Roan and Chet to get in before peeling away from the curb.

"You have to get your fear and anger under control, Justin. You can't think straight if your emotions are taking over," Roan stated calmly. "We are going to find our mate and bring her back, but you have to get your wolf to back off."

"How the fuck am I supposed to do that when that fucker has our mate in his clutches? He's already stabbed her once. God knows what he'll do to her this time, what he's doing to her right now."

"We are just as scared and torn up as you are. You're letting your imagination run away with you, Justin. Jarrod was going to call us as soon as Malcolm called in. You know as well as we do that Long is still on the move. You have to start thinking logically," Chet said. "Come on, bro, take a few deep breaths and calm down."

Justin knew his brothers were right. He concentrated on calming the turmoil roiling in his gut and pushing his wolf back down so he had better control of his emotions. When he was able to think more clearly, he prayed to God Sam was okay.

* * * *

Opening her eyes and then squinting against the light as it penetrated her retinas, she tried to focus her gaze while licking her dry lips. She had a nasty taste in her mouth, and her tongue felt like it was glued to the roof of her mouth.

Looking down she realized she was lying on a bed, and, being careful not to alert her captor she was awake, she looked about. She ascertained she was in some sort of open-plan vacation cabin.

Gerard was sitting in an armchair across the room and looked like he was reading the paper. Her gaze skittered about the room, looking for a weapon she could use to aid her in her own escape. There wasn't much in the place, but her eyes landed on a lamp near the armchair as well as a candlestick on the small dining table. There was a small kitchen off to one side, which could hold carving knives. If she were able to get up and about, she might be able to use one of those items.

Shifting quietly and minimally so as not to alert Gerard she was conscious, she nearly groaned with frustration when she realized her hands and ankles were bound. Looking down to her wrists, she saw there was duct tape wrapped around them.

Shit, what are you going to do now, Sam? Come on, girl, don't just lie there scared out of your wits. Start using the brain God gave you and think of a way out of this!

A noise across the room alerted her, and she looked up to see Gerard staring at her as he placed the paper on the coffee table.

"Hello, Sam. I'm so glad you decided to wake up and join me. We are going to have such fun together. I have waited for you for months, and nothing and no one is going to stop me now. Not even those three men you're living with, you little whore. You know, you really surprised me when you moved in with them after only just meeting them. I thought you had more morals. Just goes to show, no one is what they seem on the outside. You're a little slut just like all the others were. Peter obviously knew what he was about when he dumped your ugly ass."

Sam whimpered as he rose and stalked toward her. She could see evil intent and insanity in the depths of those blue eyes, and he scared the crap out of her. Using her hands even though her wrists were bound, she pushed and scuttled back across the bed. It was a difficult undertaking, but the farther away from him she was the better. The false security didn't last long, because before she knew it, her back was to the wall and he was standing before her, his thighs touching the mattress.

Sam cursed the fact that she hadn't told her mates she loved them when they meant the world to her. She had been so stupid, and now she didn't know if she would ever get the chance to tell them.

Closing her eyes as he reached out toward her, she flinched, waiting for the pain to begin. She had already had a taste of his violence and knew that had only been the tip of the iceberg. He reached over and grabbed her breasts in a painful grip. She bucked away from him, moisture in her eyes that he was touching her when that right belonged only to her mates, the men she loved with her whole being.

Fear permeated her soul when he pulled his hands away and reached for the knife strapped in a sheath on his belt. His eyes were so cold. Now that he had her all alone, a long thin blade in his hand, she knew she was done for.

Chapter Thirteen

"I'm going to see if I can contact Sam through our link again," Roan said just as Justin's cell phone rang.

"Hold that thought, Roan," Justin replied and then answered his cell, putting it on loud speaker. "Jarrod, what have you got?"

"Malcolm followed them to the rental cabins about ten miles this side of Nageezi. Looks like Long had it all planned out. He's going to scout the area and will meet you out front. He'll be looking out for you, but he has my orders to go in and get your mate out if you don't get there in time. Malcolm will keep me informed, and just make sure you do as he says so you don't go putting your sorry asses in danger."

"We're not stupid, Jarrod. We have been involved in pack security before, and we know what we're doing."

"Yeah, yeah, I know, but from what I've heard from the other newly mated pack members, including our Alphas, it's different when it's your mate. You're too involved to think clearly. Just watch your backs," Jarrod said.

"We will. Thanks, cousin." Justin ended the call.

"According to the GPS we're only five minutes from the rental cabins. When you get close, turn the lights off, Justin. No need to alert Long that we have him in our sights. There is no way I want that fucker escaping. He's going down one way or another," Roan said in a deep, garbled, growling voice.

"Your wolf is showing, Roan. Get control," Justin said in a calm voice, glad he was finally back in charge of his emotions. "You don't want to go off half-cocked and have your wolf take over. The last thing we need is for Malcolm to have to call the coroner and trying to explain a wolf attack."

"There's Malcolm's car," Chet pointed out as Justin killed the lights and coasted the truck to a stop.

Roan was the first one out, his brothers quickly following. He took a step toward the cabins he could see a hundred yards ahead just as Malcolm came out of the trees off to the side of the driveway.

"What can you tell us?" Justin asked.

"He has her in the first cabin. Her ankles and wrists are restrained and she's unconscious, but your mate doesn't look like she's injured," Malcolm explained. "There is only one entrance besides a couple of windows. He's reading the paper."

"Let's go."

Roan took the lead, and when they were outside the cabin he looked at his brothers. They gave a nod just before Sam's scream reached his ears.

He didn't hesitate. He kicked the door to the cabin open and scanned the interior. Sam was bound to the bed, every muscle straining away from the man looming over her. Gerard turned toward the sound of the door slamming into the wall. Roan took in the knife in the man's hand and leaped forward.

He threw himself between the knife and his mate, and the metal of the blade slashed into the flesh of his arm. Roan barely felt it. With adrenaline running through his system and his wolf empowering him, he shoved Long back with a mighty push.

Watching dispassionately, Long went careening into the far wall. He bounced off it, and then his momentum sent him tumbling forward. As he hit the floor, the knife clattered free of his grip. With a deranged snarl, Gerard lurched toward the knife. Justin dove toward it at the same moment.

Gerard's hand closed around the knife. Roan was dimly aware of Chet speaking to Sam behind him, but he couldn't take his eyes from the action. Justin threw himself on top of Long, eliciting a grunt from the madman. He couldn't quite reach the knife clasped in Long's sweaty grip, though. Roan wanted to jump in but was afraid of making matters worse.

Justin rolled onto his back, taking Gerard with him, moving far faster and more efficiently than any human could. For a moment, Long was on top of him, his arms waving as he tried to twist free of Justin's strong hold. Then Justin rolled them again so that he was on top.

Roan looked for the knife. At the same instant that he realized it was underneath Long, the human let out a strangled gasp.

Justin rolled to his feet, looking down. Gerard Long flopped on the floor, his hands scrabbling ineffectively at the blade of his own knife, embedded in his chest.

His eyes widened in shock, his mouth opened, and he gasped. In the next instant he lay still, his face twisted in a grimace of pain. He stared at nothing with unseeing eyes. As far as Roan was concerned, poetic justice had been delivered.

Turning toward Sam, he rushed to her side just as Chet removed the tape from her limbs. He scanned her body, looking for blood and injuries. His breath left in a great rush. His mate looked to be unscathed.

"Are you all right, honey? Did he hurt you?" Justin asked as he ran his hands over her body, checking for injuries.

"N—No. Y—You were j—just in t—time," Sam sobbed.

Justin pulled Sam onto his lap and embraced her. She sank her face against his chest, clutched his T-shirt in her fists, and cried. Roan moved into one side of her and rubbed his hand up and down her back, trying to offer comfort, and Chet did the same from her other side.

When the storm had finally passed, Roan scooped Sam up into his arms and inhaled her familiar scent. Her limbs were still shaking as the adrenaline coursing through her system looked for an out, but then he realized she wasn't the only one shaking. He sank down onto the side of the bed and buried his face in her hair, against her neck. He breathed deeply. His wolf backed off when he didn't smell any blood on his mate, and he exhaled on a sigh of relief.

"Are you sure you're okay, sweetheart?" asked Roan.

"Yes, I'm fine. Can we go home now?" Sam lifted her head, her tears finally abating, looking from him to Chet and Justin and finally to the floor of the cabin. Malcolm was standing over the corpse, shaking his head slightly. His radio squawked, and Roan knew the place would soon be overrun with police.

"Are we done here, Malcolm?" Chet inquired.

"Yeah, we're done for now. I'll come by the house later to get your mate's statement. I have to hang around for the coroner. It's nice to finally meet you, Samantha. I only wish it was under different circumstances."

"Me, too."

Roan stood with Sam in his arms and headed out. He carried her to the truck and got into the backseat with her. After buckling her in, he sat right next to her, his arm wrapped around her shoulders. She leaned into his side with her head resting against his chest and snuggled up. Moments later her breathing evened out and she fell asleep.

"How's our mate doing?" Justin asked as he glanced up in the rearview mirror.

"She's asleep. She's totally exhausted. I think I would be, too, if I'd been through what she has," Roan replied.

"As soon as we get home we'll put her to bed. Our Alphas are going to want an account from us, but I don't want Sam left alone for a minute. She's going to need all our attention and love to get over this," Chet said.

"Shit, it nearly tore my heart out when she started crying. She's had to be so strong for a long time and with no one to lean on. I don't ever want her to be in such danger again. I'm just glad it's finally over, and hopefully she can put this all behind her."

"I can't believe her ex-husband did that to her. The fucking bastard!" Roan snarled. "If I ever lay eyes on him, I am going to rip him apart piece by piece. How that fucker could ever tell Sam she was ugly is beyond me. The guy must be blind."

* * * *

Jolting awake to the sound of screaming, she bolted upright in bed only to slump when she realized she was safe. The bedside light was switched on. Three sets of hands ran over her body with soothing motions, and three sets of eyes looked at her with concern.

"Are you okay, honey?" Justin asked from beside her.

"Yes. I'm sorry I woke you all," she answered huskily. Her throat was slightly sore, and she knew she must have screamed really loudly. A banging noise from a door slamming open echoed in the silence, and then there were nine large men trying to see into the bedroom.

Sam shrank down and pulled the quilt up over her chest, thankful that she actually had a T-shirt covering her breasts. Usually she slept nude, and even though she was confused, at this moment she was actually grateful for the clothes.

"What's going on? We heard screaming," Jonah asked.

Sam's cheeks heated with embarrassment at having screamed loud enough to wake the whole house. The place was massive. No wonder her throat was hurting her.

"Everything's fine. Sam just had a nightmare. Thanks for coming to check on her," Justin replied.

"I'm sorry." Sam lowered her eyes to the bed.

"Don't worry about it, honey," Jonah said. "We're all glad that you're back home where you belong, safe and sound with your mates. Try and get some more rest. Come on, guys, let's leave them be." They all left again.

"Oh God." Sam covered her face with her hands. "I can't believe they all heard me."

"Shh, honey. Don't get upset. You weren't that loud. We can hear the slightest sound, Sam. Our wolves pick up so much more than humans do." Justin pulled her into his arms.

"Do you want to talk about your bad dream, sweetheart?" Roan inquired.

"No. I have to get up. I need to shower." She pushed against Justin's hold on her.

"Darlin', you're safe here. No one will hurt you," Chet told her, running a hand up and down her quilt-covered thigh.

"I know that. I'm sorry. I just need to wash his touch away. I feel so dirty," she sobbed.

"Take it easy, honey. We'll get you cleaned up."

Justin pulled the covers off her, lifted her into his arms, and carried her to the bathroom. While he stripped her down, Roan turned on the faucet to the large spa bath and Chet put some of her favorite bath salts into the water. Checking the temperature to make sure it was to her liking, Justin once again lifted her and stepped into the tub, sitting down in the blissfully warm water and pulling her onto his lap.

"Just sit back and relax, darlin'." Chet picked up a sponge. "We'll get you clean."

"Hurry. I can still smell him on me," Sam urged with a hitch in her voice.

"Look at me, honey," Justin demanded, and she looked up, meeting his gaze without any hesitation. "I love you, Sam. You're safe. He can't ever hurt you again."

"He's dead, baby," Roan added.

Sam felt a curious lack of relief. Realizing why, she said, "Peter is still out there, though." She lifted her gaze to each of her men in turn. "He seems to have forgotten about me for now, but what if—?"

"Shh, sweetheart. We've got it all taken care of," Chet said.

"Chet," Justin grumbled in warning.

Sam looked between them again. "What do you mean?"

Roan explained, "We know the local pack near Sebring. Justin sent an e-mail this morning to one of their Betas. If Peter ever contacts you again or spreads nasty rumors about you, he won't know what hit him."

"We weren't going to tell you," Justin added. "We don't want you to worry about it at all."

"I won't." Saying the words, Sam felt something lift from her shoulders. She was safe now.

Resting her head against Justin's shoulder, she closed her eyes and relished the caresses to her body as Roan and Chet began to wash her. She felt so comforted and right, being with her mates. She loved them so much, and they loved her in return. Every time they looked at her she could see the love they felt for her shining from the depths of their eyes.

Once her body was clean and she could no longer smell Gerard's stench on her, she relaxed for the first time since waking so abruptly. Roan and Chet moved in on her sides, and she looked at Roan when he gently pulled her face around to his. He placed an emotion-filled, gentle kiss against her lips, and she sighed as she met his gaze.

"I love you, sweetheart, so much. You were meant to be here with us. I would give my life for you, Sam."

Chet cupped her chin and turned her head toward him. His eyes looked to be glistening with moisture as he stared deeply into her gaze. "I love you, darlin'. I couldn't continue breathing if you weren't here with us."

"Oh God. I don't know what I ever did to deserve any of you, but I am so glad that I ended up in Aztec. I love you all so damn much, it hurts," Sam sobbed and reached out her arms and wrapped them around Roan's and Chet's necks as she snuggled into Justin's big body, too.

"You have no idea how long we've been waiting to hear you say that, honey." Justin kissed and licked along her shoulder. "Are you feeling better now, Sam?"

"Yes."

"Are you up for some loving, sweetheart?" asked Roan.

"God yes. Please? I love you all so much. I need you to make love with me. I need your hands and mouths on me."

"We are gonna love you so good, darlin'. Let's get you out of the tub and dried off," Chet said and easily scooped her up into his arms and out of the tub.

Sam stood still and let her men dry her, and when they were done Roan carried her back into the bedroom. Her pussy clenched and leaked cream as she admired the naked, muscular bodies of the men she loved more than any other person in the world. She couldn't wait for the loving to begin.

Chapter Fourteen

"We are going to spend the rest of the night loving on you, darlin'," Chet rasped in a deep cadence as he climbed onto the bed.

Sam was in the center of the mattress, her breath panting rapidly in and out between her lips, her chest rising and falling with excited desire. Her gaze connected with each of her mates', and her heart lurched in her chest to see all the love they felt for her exposed to her eyes. She felt so full of happiness and joy, so complete where she had felt so empty and lonely for so long. She looked forward to loving her men for the rest of her days.

Chet watched her like she was prey to his predator, and her pussy gushed out more of her cream in preparation for some loving from her men. Crawling up between her thighs, he gently pried them apart, caressing her legs, the palms of his hands going higher and higher until they were barely an inch away from her weeping pussy. He never took his eyes from her as he slowly lowered his head to the apex of her thighs. The first lick of his tongue on her clit made her demand more with the arch of her hips. She bucked up into his mouth, needing to feel more of his touch. She cried out in animalistic need when Chet's tongue slid down through her folds and pushed into her cunt.

Looking over to Roan when he cupped her cheek, she sighed in bliss when he leaned in and kissed her. The meeting of their mouths started off gentle and slow and so full of emotion that tears pricked her eyeballs. She closed her eyes as he deepened the kiss, and her body began to go up in flames. When the mattress dipped on her other side, she knew Justin had finally joined them on the bed. She sobbed into Roan's mouth when Justin sucked on her nipple.

"You are so fucking gorgeous, honey," Justin rumbled against her flesh, the vibrations shooting from her breast straight down to her pussy and causing her internal muscles to clench. "I will never be able to get enough of you, Sam."

Sam cried out, in awe of the fact that her mates already had her on the verge of an orgasm. Her womb felt heavy, and molten lava was running through her body. Bucking up and whimpering when Chet removed his mouth from her pussy, she tried to stay in contact with his mouth. He gave a slight chuckle.

"Please?" she begged.

"Please what, darlin'?" he asked.

"I need you to love me. I want all of you filling me up."

"Shh, just relax, Sam. We'll take care of you. You are so sexy and full of fire. I can't wait to have my cock buried in your pretty little pussy," Chet panted.

"Now!"

"We control what happens in the bedroom, honey. You don't get to tell us what to do. Remember?" Justin asked.

"But I need you all so much."

"And we need you, too, sweetness. Just lie back and relax," Roan rumbled in a voice so deep it was almost a growl.

Sam's breaths were coming so hard and fast in her excitement that she felt totally out of control, but it was nice to know she wasn't the only one affected.

Chet moved up onto his knees between her thighs, and then he was slowly pushing his big cock into her pussy. Reaching out with her arms, intent on grabbing his hips and pulling him in faster, she whimpered with frustration when Roan and Justin each took hold of her wrists and pulled them up above her head, pinning them to the mattress.

"Nice and slow, darlin'," Chet crooned to her. "I don't want to hurt you, Sam."

"You won't. Please, I just need you to fuck me, hard."

Justin and Roan each ran their hands all over her body. She wasn't sure if they were trying to inflame her libido or calm it down, but she didn't care. All she wanted was to have them filling all of her. She was so on edge, and Chet was taking his time penetrating her. She'd had just about more torture than she could stand. Wrapping her legs around his hips, she used her muscles, tightening her limbs around him and bucking up, moaning with pleasure as his hard cock slid into her pussy until his balls connected with her ass.

"Fuck, you feel so good, darlin'. You are a naughty girl, Sam. We'll have to punish you for that later," Chet groaned but held still inside her. He looked at Roan and Justin.

The other two men moved away from her, and then in a lightning-fast move, Chet rolled over, ending up on his back with her lying over him, her thighs spread wide outside of his.

"Don't you move, honey. I'm just going to prepare your ass so we can all love you together," Justin said in a deep, rumbling voice.

Sam mewled and tried to rock her hips when Justin began to caress her anus with lubed fingers. She relaxed her muscles like they had taught her and pushed back against him.

"You're such a greedy little thing, aren't you, honey. Fuck, your ass is gripping my fingers so hard."

"Don't move, sweetheart," Roan growled and popped her ass cheek.

The heat from his smack travelled to her ass and pussy, only firing her arousal to a higher level. It felt so carnally erotic to have Chet's cock in her pussy while Justin began to fuck his fingers in and out of her bottom.

She moaned and clenched around his digits as he withdrew them from her back entrance.

"Are you ready, honey?"

"Yes!" She screamed her reply. "Hurry! Please."

Justin covered her back, his chest hair tickling her skin, and then she groaned as his cock began to penetrate her rosette. Squeezing her eyes closed tightly, she savored the burning and pinching sensation as his cock worked its way into her back channel. He took his time, thrusting in short, sharp digs, letting her body adjust slowly to his invasion. Swiveling her hips and trying to get him to go faster only earned Sam another smack to her butt.

"Stop moving, Sam, or it's going to be over before we even start," Justin rasped. "Hold her still."

Chet wrapped his arms around her waist to prevent her from moving too much, and Roan placed a hand between her shoulder blades while Justin gripped her hips firmly.

"Not so squirmy now, are you, honey?" Justin said with a chuckle, and then he groaned when she used her pelvic-floor muscles to clench on the cocks sheathed in her body.

"Fuck, you feel so good, darlin'," Chet moaned.

"Okay, I'm in."

Sam sobbed as Justin and Chet moved her into a sitting position, her torso perpendicular to Chet's. Roan reached over, cupping her cheek in his large palm, and turned her toward him. Her gaze locked onto his cock, which was at eye level as he knelt on the bed next to her. The sexy bastard was stroking his hand up and down his hard shaft, and she could see drops of pre-cum glistening on the tip. Leaning slightly to the side, she licked her lips just before she opened her mouth and engulfed the head of his dick.

"Oh yeah. That's it, sweetness, suck my cock. Your mouth feels like heaven, sweetheart," Roan gasped.

Whimpering with delight and pleasure around Roan's cock when Justin pulled his cock from her ass and surged back in, she tried to follow his movement by thrusting her hips. But between him and Chet there was no way she could move. She growled with frustration, but that only made her men laugh huskily.

She groaned as pleasure zinged from her pussy to her ass and back again when Justin and Chet began to counterthrust in and out of her holes. She laved her tongue on the underside of Roan's cock then bobbed up and down his length. Juices leaked continuously from her excited pussy as she tried to suck Roan to the back of her throat. She gagged once then breathed deeply through her nose and tried again. This time she succeeded in taking him farther down her throat and swallowed around the head of his cock.

"Fuck! You are incredible, sweetheart. Do that again," Roan demanded.

So she did. Sam whimpered and gasped when Chet and Justin began to fuck her harder. The friction of the erections sliding in and out of her body had her teetering on the verge of climax. Her toes curled as tingling warmth traversed her pussy and limbs. The wave coiling up inside her was so big, it almost scared her at its size, but Roan's groan and words helped to calm her and let their love wash over her.

"I'm coming, Sam."

He roared out his release, and she swallowed quickly, making sure she took every drop of his cum down her throat. She cleaned him up before he pulled from her mouth and collapsed on the bed beside her, still breathing heavily.

"Oh my God. It's too good," she panted.

"No, honey. It'll never be too good," Justin replied as he thrust back into her ass.

"Come, darlin'." Chet growled his demand, slipped a finger down between their bodies, and tapped her clit.

That one touch was all it took for the wave to break over her. She screamed with orgasmic bliss as wave after wave of rapture washed over her, making her body shake from the top of her head to the tips of her curled toes.

"That's it, honey. I can feel your ass milking the cum from my balls," Justin groaned.

And then Justin slammed into her ass one more time and roared out. His cock swelled and jerked in her ass as he climaxed, his seed spewing into her channel. The warm bursts only seemed to enhance her own orgasm, sending another round of contractions running through her womb and pussy. Moments later, Chet held her hips firmly, thrust his cock into her rippling cunt, and froze, shouting out as he reached his own release and filled her with his cum.

"You are so fucking sexy, sweetheart," Roan stated in a husky voice. He pushed the damp hair from her face where she rested her cheek on Chet's chest. "I love you, Sam."

"Me, too." She sighed out her reply and smiled, too satiated to open her eyes.

"You are gorgeous, honey. Love you." Justin's voice held so much emotion that it brought tears to her eyes.

"Ditto," she mumbled, finally opening her eyes when he kissed her nape.

"You are so special, darlin'. You mean the world to me," Chet exclaimed, gently lifting her head up and kissing her lips.

"I love you, too. All of you. I'm sorry I didn't say those words earlier. I was scared. It took Gerard's kidnapping to open my eyes. Life is too uncertain and short to be afraid. I won't let fear stand in my way again." Sam groaned when Chet eased his cock from her pussy.

When she went to move, Justin wrapped his arms around her waist and rolled them both onto their sides. "Stay right where you are, honey. We'll take care of you."

Roan must have slipped into the bathroom when she hadn't been looking. He climbed onto the bed and lifted her leg, cleaning her pussy and ass, and Chet patted her with a dry towel.

"There you go, sweetheart. Relax and close your eyes. You need a good night's rest. We have a surprise for you tomorrow."

Even though Sam had heard Roan and was curious, her men had totally worn her out, and she was already starting to fall asleep. She planned to question them first thing in the morning about their surprise. She absolutely loved surprises.

Chapter Fifteen

Sam woke with an air of expectancy because she remembered Roan had said something about a surprise right before she had fallen asleep. Stretching and smiling, she opened her eyes only to find herself alone in bed. Her smile turned to a frown, but she got up and went to shower and dress.

By the time she headed downstairs to find her men, she wasn't feeling very happy anymore. She hated waking up alone, and she had told her mates countless times how much she enjoyed waking up with them beside her.

Stomping into the kitchen, she helped Angie and Cindy take the plates of food to the table and glared at Justin, Roan, and Chet when they smiled at her. She backtracked a little when she remembered what they had said about challenging them in front of the pack. Taking a deep breath, she exhaled slowly and counted to ten then lowered her eyes, turned, and headed back to the kitchen for more food.

Sitting down to breakfast, she only picked at her food and wouldn't look at her mates. She jumped when two large hands landed on her thighs and lightly brushed over her.

"What's the matter, honey?" asked Justin.

"Nothing," she replied with a grumble.

"Did you get out of bed on the wrong side, darlin'?" Chet leaned toward her from her other side.

"No!" she snapped.

"Are you sure there's nothing wrong, sweetheart?" Roan was sitting beside Justin.

Sam finally lifted her head and frowned at them, but instead of answering she shook her head slightly then looked back down at her plate. It wasn't just that she had woken alone that was making her grumpy, and if she was honest with herself, she really had no idea why she was feeling so cranky.

Hearing Justin sniff the air and then Chet, she felt even more confused when they leaned into her and smelled her neck. Roan got up from his chair and came to stand behind her. He, too, leaned in and breathed in against her skin.

"You smell so good, Sam," Roan said in a deep, grumbling voice.

She lifted her head and turned to frown at him, but as she did she caught every male in the room surreptitiously smelling the air. Frowning again, Sam lifted her arm and sniffed her pit. No, she didn't smell. She'd just had a shower for God's sake. *What the hell is going on?*

All of a sudden the men began to howl and cheer and started congratulating her mates. She had no idea what was going on, but her men seemed pleased about something. Their chests were puffed up as if they had achieved something spectacularly masculine.

Looking over to first Michelle, then Keira, and lastly Talia, she found each of them smiling back at her as if they knew a secret. She opened her mouth, but Justin leaned in and kissed her passionately right there in front of everyone. Her cheeks were warm, and when he finally lifted his mouth from her, she knew the pack members would see her embarrassment.

"Justin…"

Roan bent down over her shoulder, covering her mouth with his, and swallowed the rest of her sentence. When he was done and had pulled away she looked at her mates with bewilderment. Her gaze met Chet's, and he slowly reached up, threading his fingers through her hair, holding her still as he lowered his lips to hers. By the time he was finished, she was breathing heavily and horny as hell.

"Come on, honey, we need to show you something," Justin said, taking her hand and leading her from the room.

"What's going on? Why weren't you in bed when I woke up?" she asked moodily.

"We'll explain it all to you in a moment, sweetheart," Roan replied and scooped her up into his arms.

Sam wrapped her arms around his neck and leaned into him. Inhaling his masculine scent, she couldn't resist taking a taste. Licking up and down the side of his neck, she heard a growl rumble against her side and loved that she could affect her men just as much as they affected her. Nibbling on his earlobe, she giggled when he groaned and pulled her in tighter against him.

She had been so wrapped up in what she was doing, she hadn't taken any notice of where they were going, and when she did she wasn't really surprised to find them back in the bedroom.

Her breath caught in her throat when the scent of roses wafted to her nostrils, and the sight before her brought tears to her eyes.

"Oh my. That is so beautiful," she gasped and sniffed when moisture formed in her eyes. "How and when did you do this?"

Their bedroom had lit candles on every surface and rose petals were strewn across the bed and on the floor. An ice bucket with a bottle of champagne sat on one of the bedside tables as well as four glasses.

"Cindy and Angie snuck up here to set it up for us once the food had been served. We wanted to surprise you."

Roan lowered her down his body until her feet connected with the bed, and he held her steady while helping her to sit on the edge. He looked at his brothers, and then as one they all knelt down at her feet. Roan was holding one of her hands, and Justin reached out to take the other. Chet placed his palm on her thigh and rubbed gently.

"Sam, you mean the world to us, and we would be honored if you would agree to marry us. Will you marry us, darlin'?" Chet asked.

"I thought we were already married," Sam said, a little confused. "You told me that when you bit and marked me I was your wife."

"You are, sweetheart, don't ever doubt that. We would like to be married to you on paper as well," Roan explained.

"Honey, we love you so damn much. We want to make sure you are looked after if anything ever happens to us. We decided since I am the eldest you will marry me on paper, and if something does happen then you will have our name. We will be able to legally look after you. Please, marry us, Samantha?"

"Yes! God yes! I love you all so much. I would be honored to marry you all," she replied, reaching out, touching each of her mates on the face as tears of joy ran down her cheeks.

Chet reached into his shirt pocket and withdrew a small jeweler's box. Opening it, he held it out to Justin. Gasping with awe, she eyed the two-carat diamond solitaire set in gold with two smaller diamonds on either side and watched Justin pluck the ring from the box. He placed the ring on her left hand, and Sam swore she felt a circle of warmth around her finger.

"It's so beautiful. I love you all so damn much. I can't wait to marry you, have babies with you, and grow old with you." She sobbed joyfully.

"We already have a head start on the baby, darlin'," Chet said with an exuberant grin.

"What?"

"You're pregnant, sweetheart," Roan said gently and winked at her.

"How do you…?"

"Honey, we're werewolves, remember?" Justin interrupted, tapping his nose. "We smelled the change in your scent this morning. You conceived our baby last night."

Sam launched herself from the bed and into the waiting arms of her mates. If anyone had told her a couple of months ago she would be pregnant and mated to three hot, sexy werewolves, she would have told them they were delusional.

She felt so complete and full of love, and nothing was going get in between her and her men, ever. Sam couldn't wait to hold her baby in her arms, and she looked forward to spending long, love-filled years with the loves of her life.

THE END

WWW.BECCAVAN-EROTICROMANCE.COM

ABOUT THE AUTHOR

My name is Becca Van. I live in Australia with my wonderful hubby of many years, as well as my two children.

I read my first romance, which I found in the school library, at the age of thirteen and haven't stopped reading them since. It is so wonderful to know that love is still alive and strong when there seems to be so much conflict in the world.

I dreamed of writing my own book one day but unfortunately didn't follow my dream for many years. But once I started I knew writing was what I wanted to continue doing.

I love to escape from the world and curl up with a good romance to see how the characters unfold and conflict is dealt with. I have read many books and love all facets of the romance genre, from historical to erotic romance. I am a sucker for a happy ending.

For all titles by Becca Van, please visit
www.bookstrand.com/becca-van

Siren Publishing, Inc.
www.SirenPublishing.com

CPSIA information can be obtained at www.ICGtesting.com
Printed in the USA
LVOW09s1754220215

427898LV00026B/891/P